魚**鷹**與男孩

OPERATION OSPREY

ABOUT THIS BOOK

Structures

Sequencing of future tenses	Could / was able to / managed to
Present perfect plus *yet*, *already*, *just*	Had to / didn't have to
First conditional	Shall / could for offers
Present and past passive	May / can / could for permission Might for future possibility
How long?	Make and let
Very / really / quite	Causative have Want / ask / tell someone to do something

Structures from lower levels are also included.

CONTENTS

I was born in Walsall, a town in the area of the English Midlands known as The Black Country. I lived on the edge of the town, and I just had to cross the road to get into an enormous park, which extended right out into the open countryside.

I spent most of my free time in the park and the fields and that started my love of the natural world. Then when I was 15, my parents took me on a camping holiday to Scotland, and that was the first time that I saw the ospreys that this story is about—we visited them at the famous Loch Garten site. And a year later I joined the Royal Society for the Protection of Birds (RSPB), the birdwatching club that both of the boys in the story belong to.

When I was eighteen I went to college and made close friends with a student who went on to become a professional birdwatcher. We spent a lot of time watching birds and later he taught me how to catch them safely in nets and put rings on their legs in order to follow their movements.

After college I worked as a teacher and I also started writing poetry and short stories.

I have lived in Italy, Kosovo and Serbia and am currently living in Hungary and travel extensively throughout the world as part of my job as a freelance writer, teacher and teacher trainer. And of course wherever I go I always see something or meet someone who is an inspiration for a story or a character or an unexpected twist in my latest piece of writing.

I hope you enjoy reading the story as much as I enjoyed writing it and will be inspired to get out and look at what is happening in the countryside near you.

The story of the return of the osprey[1] to nest in Britain is amazing. Ospreys were hunted to extinction[2] by 1910. After this they were only seen as they migrated[3] to and from their nesting sites in Scandinavia and Russia. Then in 1954 a pair returned to Loch Garten in Scotland.

The RSPB set up a guard on the island under the trees where the birds had nested. Over the next few years they reared[4] a number of chicks, but some of the eggs were stolen. Eventually Loch Garten became a Bird Reserve[5] where the public could watch the birds and their chicks. Gradually, the young birds also returned and built nests on other lakes in Scotland and now there are over 100 pairs nesting each year.

Birdwatchers[6] had been waiting for the first pair to breed further south in England. In recent years osprey pairs have bred successfully in Wales and Scotland.

The osprey (Latin name: *Pandion haliaetus*) is a magnificent bird to look at. Its body is 50-60 cm long, and its wingspan[7] is 150-170 cm. One thing that makes it so interesting for birdwatchers is that, unlike most other birds of prey, the osprey eats fish. It catches them by flying high above the lake and then diving into the water, holding out its claws to catch the fish just before it hits the surface. It then holds the fish in its claws and flies out of the water to eat the fish on the branch of a tree, or at its nest.

The nest is a huge pile of sticks at the top of a tree. It is up to 1.5 meters in width, and the birds return to the same nest year after year. Ospreys migrate from Europe to sub-Saharan Africa to spend each winter, and return the following April to nest.

---

1 osprey [ˋɑsprɪ] (n.) 鶚；魚鷹
2 extinction [ɪkˋstɪŋkʃən] (n.) 滅絕
3 migrate [ˋmaɪˏgret] (v.) 遷移；移居
4 rear [rɪr] (v.) 飼養
5 reserve [rɪˋzɝv] (n.) 保護區
6 birdwatcher [ˋbɝdˏwɑtʃɚ] (n.) 野鳥觀察家；賞鳥人
7 wingspan [ˋwɪŋˏspæn] (n.) 翼幅

1 Think about the birds you know which live in your country. How many different ones can you name? See if you can write down the names of twelve birds. Do you know any of their names in English?

1 _____	2 _____	3 _____
4 _____	5 _____	6 _____
7 _____	8 _____	9 _____
10 _____	11 _____	12 _____

2 Look at the picture and write the words in the box in the correct places.

> osprey   fish   nest
> island   pine tree   lake

3 Who is who in the story? Match the descriptions to the pictures.

- a   Hello, I'm Don's dad. Don's really into birdwatching and I love looking at the pictures he takes.
- b   Hello, I'm Don Ball. I'm 15 and I love birdwatching. Oh, and I've got a quick temper, too.
- c   Hello there. I'm Sergeant Keddle. I'm the policeman in Saltley. It's usually quiet here, but then Mike and Don discovered something interesting.
- d   Hi, I'm Mike Peters, I'm 15 and I'm Don's best friend. I've got blond hair and my most prized possession is my binoculars.

4 Think and discuss. The osprey is an endangered species. What other endangered species do you know in the world? Why do animals, plants and birds become endangered? What happens when an animal, plant or bird becomes extinct? Do you know the names of any extinct wildlife? What can people do to prevent endangered species from becoming extinct?

5 The title of this book is "Operation Osprey". What do you think the story is going to be about?

❶ A text invitation

I was coming home from school on the bus on Tuesday, when I got a text message[1] from Mike. It was very short: Mkt X 7. UGNT. I knew that this meant he wanted to meet me at the Market Cross[2] at seven o'clock that evening and that it was something urgent.

It was also a bit[3] unusual. We'd arranged[4] to meet after school on Friday to plan our weekend's birdwatching[5] as usual, so this must be something special. I felt excited!

Let me give you some background. My name's Don Ball. I'm fifteen and I go to Blueway Comprehensive School[6]. Mike (or Mike Peters, to give him his full name) is the same age and goes to the local grammar school[7], but we've been friends since junior school[8]. We both live in the village of Saltley, which is in the Midlands.

We've been birdwatching together since we were 11. I suppose[9] we're quite good at[10] it now, because we do it regularly[11], read about it, use the Net[12] to find out about birds, and we're members of a club for birdwatchers, too.

1 text message 手機簡訊	7 grammar school〔英〕普通高中
2 cross [krɔs] (n.) 十字形	8 junior school〔英〕小學
3 a bit 有一點兒	9 suppose [sə`poz] (v.) 認為應該
4 arrange [ə`rendʒ] (v.) 安排	10 be good at 擅長……
5 birdwatching [`bɝdwɑtʃɪŋ] (n.) 賞鳥	11 regularly [`rɛgjələlɪ] (adv.) 經常地
6 comprehensive school 綜合中學	12 Net [nɛt] (n.) 網際網路

> ## THINK
>
> - What do you think Mike is going to tell Don when they meet?

When I got home, I got some biscuits and orange juice and went up to my room to get on with[1] my homework so that I could go out and meet Mike later. It took me longer than usual to do it because my mind kept wandering[2], thinking of what Mike wanted to tell me. He must have seen an unusual bird. (Of course, I thought his text message must be because of a bird!!)

It was early April and birds which had gone south to warmer countries for the winter were coming back to Britain for the summer now. We were looking forward to[3] "meeting old friends" . . . but there was always the chance of something rare[4] and unusual arriving, too.

---

1 get on with 馬上進行……
2 wander [ˋwɑndə] (v.) 漫遊
3 look forward to 期待（後接名詞或動名詞）
4 rare [rɛr] (a.) 稀有的
5 pub [pʌb] (n.) 酒吧
6 grocer's [ˋgrosəz] (n.) 食品雜貨商
7 commute [kəˋmjut] (v.) 通勤
8 square [skwɛr] (n.) 廣場
9 well-known [ˋwɛlˋnon] (a.) 眾所周知的
10 meeting-place [ˋmitɪŋˋples] (n.) 相約見面的地方
11 lapwing [ˋlæp͵wɪŋ] (n.) 田鳧
12 whistle [ˋhwɪsl] (n.) 口哨聲
13 mysteriously [mɪsˋtɪrɪəslɪ] (adv.) 神祕兮兮地
14 bench [bɛntʃ] (n.) 長椅
15 impatient [ɪmˋpeʃənt] (a.) 無耐心的

❷ Hearing the news

At 6.45, I left the house and walked down the road to the center of the village. Saltley is a small place. There's an old church, two pubs[5], a post office, a grocer's[6] and a couple of other general shops.

It's home to about 1000 people—half of them work on the nearby farms and the other half commute[7] to the nearest big city to work. And right in the middle of the small square[8] in the center of Saltley stands the Market Cross, which is a well-known[9] meeting-place[10] for everyone from the area.

I said hello to several people I knew as I walked over to sit on the steps at the base of the stone cross.

Soon I heard Mike's familiar lapwing[11] whistle[12], and saw him standing on the other side of the road. I walked over.

"Hi, Mike. What's this about?" I asked at once.

"Just wait a moment until we're away from the crowd and I'll tell you," he answered mysteriously[13].

We walked over to the church yard and sat on one of the benches[14].

"So?" I asked again.

"Oooh, you're so impatient[15]!" he joked, but I could tell that he was excited, too.

I waited. He began.

"I took the day off[1] school today," he said. "After this week of good weather followed by last night's storm, I thought there might be some good birds about."

"And were there?" I asked.

"Well, there are some nice new arrivals[2]—a few swallows[3], a chiffchaff[4] calling," he answered. "But then I went to RP."

RP was the name we gave to a set of three small lakes surrounded[5] by woods. They were labeled Redman's Pools on large-scale[6] maps, but lots of people didn't know they were there because they were hidden by trees.

I waited again. A smile played over Mike's face.

"Osprey," he said very quietly.

"What!?" I shouted.

"Osprey," he said again, simply.

I sat staring at him with my mouth open.

I should explain. An osprey is a big hunting bird, which catches fish. It's really spectacular[7] when it dives[8] into the water feet first and catches a big fish and flies off with it.

There weren't any in Britain[9] because they'd been hunted too much, but then in 1954 a pair nested[10] in Loch Garten in Scotland. They were protected[11] by the RSPB, because lots of people wanted the eggs for their collections. But now they've spread[12] to nest at lots of lakes around Scotland. People hope that they will soon start nesting all over England, too.

We'd never seen an osprey at RP before, and I'd never seen one at all. Mike had seen one when he'd been on a birdwatching trip to Scotland last summer. I was jealous.

"I watched it for more than an hour. It flew[13] in from the trees on Castle Hill. I knew something was coming because all the ducks flew away," he said. "And then it circled[14] over Big Pool twice, and sat in the pine trees on the island in the middle. It flew away to the west."

We were silent—he was thinking about what he'd seen and I was thinking what I had missed while I'd been sitting in my maths[15] class that afternoon.

After a time, Mike said: "So, shall we go to RP tomorrow morning?"

"But I've got school", I said.

"So have I," he said. "Just like today."

"But do you think it'll be there?" I asked.

1　day off 休假日
2　arrival [əˋraɪvl̩] (n.) 新到的人或物
3　swallow [ˋswɑlo] (n.) 燕子
4　chiffchaff [ˋtʃɪf͵tʃæf] (n.) 棕柳鶯
5　surround [səˋraʊnd] (v.) 圍繞
6　large-scale [ˋlɑrdʒˋskel] (a.) 大比例尺的
7　spectacular [spɛkˋtækjələ˞] (a.) 壯觀的
8　dive [daɪv] (v.) 跳水；潛水；俯衝
9　Britain [ˋbrɪtən] (n.) 英國
10　nest [nɛst] (v.) 築巢
11　protect [prəˋtɛkt] (v.) 保護
12　spread [sprɛd] (v.) 散布（動詞三態：spread; spread; spread）
13　fly [flaɪ] (v.) 飛（動詞三態：fly; flew; flown）
14　circle [ˋsɝkl̩] (v.) 盤旋
15　maths [mæθs] (n.) 數學（= mathematics）

"Birdwatcher!" he said. By which he meant that if I was a birdwatcher, I should know that nobody could say what a bird would or wouldn't do at a particular time, especially when they were migrating.

"So, are you coming?"

"Oh . . . oh . . . alright," I said, knowing my parents would be very angry if they found out. They already thought I spent too much time birdwatching and not enough time studying.

❸ Time off school

I was afraid to take the whole day off school, so I went in the morning. Once I was in school I pretended[1] to be ill and was sent home.

As I took the bus back to the village I felt very excited, and a little nervous. I got off at the stop near the entrance[2] to the hidden track[3] that leads down to the pools. I took my binoculars[4] out of my school bag and hung them around my neck ready to use.

I met Mike, as planned, near the disused[5] buildings of Redman's Farm, and we sat on a gate which let us look over Big Pool.

"Have you seen anything yet?" I asked, and he read me the list from his notebook—a mixture of water birds and other small birds. But osprey was not amongst them. We scanned[6] the pool, calling out the names of the species[7] of duck and other birds we could see.

"Let's walk around the other two pools," I suggested.

I hid my heavy school bag behind a large stone and we set off[8] round the northern side of Big Pool, and then through the trees to the smaller Marsh[9] Pool. There we added some more species to our list, including some grey herons[10].

---

1 pretend [prɪˋtɛnd] (v.) 假裝
2 entrance [ˋɛntrəns] (n.) 入口
3 track [træk] (n.) 小徑
4 binoculars [bɪˋnɑkjələs] (n.) 〔複〕雙筒望遠鏡
5 disused [dɪsˋjuzd] (a.) 廢棄不用的

6 scan [skæn] (v.) 瀏覽
7 species [ˋspiʃiz] (n.) 種類
8 set off 動身
9 marsh [mɑrʃ] (n.) 沼澤
10 heron [ˋhɛrən] (n.) 蒼鷺

After watching there for about half an hour, we wandered back past the third lake—Wood Pool. I was just about to say that it must have gone, when I heard a whistle from Mike.

"Look! Left island tree on Big Pool," he said in a loud whisper.

I looked, and there it was—my first osprey.

"WOW!" I shouted, as I examined the white chest, dark brown back and white head with it's brown eye-stripe[1] and yellow eye.

"Keep quiet, you idiot," said Mike quietly and angrily, "Or you'll frighten it off."

Just then the bird took off[2] from the branch[3] where it had been sitting, circled the pool and called loudly "pyep." We watched, and to our amazement[4] it was joined by another osprey which must have been sitting somewhere else.

"Two ospreys!" Mike exclaimed[5].

The birds circled the lake, calling "pyep" a few times, and then settled[6] on the pine trees on the island again.

"This is amazing," I said. "You know, they might be looking for somewhere to build a nest."

We both knew it was too much to hope for, so we said nothing.

And we left them there and went home on the bus, hoping our parents wouldn't find out what we'd been doing.

THINK

- Why was **Don** so excited when he saw the osprey?
- Can you think of a time when you were very excited about something? What was it?
- Why did the boys know that the ospreys nesting at **Redman's Pools** was "too much to hope for"?

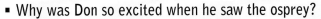
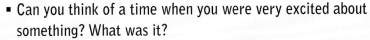

1 stripe [straɪp] (n.) 條紋	4 amazement [əˈmezmənt] (n.) 吃驚
2 take off 起飛	5 exclaim [ɪksˈklem] (v.) 驚叫
3 branch [bræntʃ] (n.) 樹枝	6 settle [ˈsɛtl̩] (v.) 棲息

❹ The holidays

Of course, we spent the whole of the following weekend watching the ospreys as they flew around gracefully and fished spectacularly in the pools, and we were very glad a week later when the Easter[1] holidays started.

We spent every day there, cycling out while it was still dark, making notes, doing drawings, taking photographs[2], recording[3] the birds' activities, and soon we realized[4] that they were starting to make a nest.

We decided that it would be better to keep the whole thing a secret because we knew there were lots of egg collectors who would like to have an osprey's egg in their collection, even though it was illegal[5]. So we said nothing to the few people we met there—the occasional[6] fisherman or walker. They never noticed the ospreys and they probably wouldn't recognize[7] them.

In the end we told my parents. Mike and I were having supper[8] with them one evening when we'd got back from a day watching our ospreys, and they asked lots of questions about what we were doing.

---

1 Easter ['istɚ] (n.) 復活節
2 photograph ['fotə,græf] (n.) 相片
3 record [rɪ'kɔrd] (v.) 記錄
4 realize ['rɪə,laɪz] (v.) 了解到
5 illegal [ɪ'ligl] (a.) 非法的
6 occasional [ə'keʒənl] (a.) 偶爾的
7 recognize ['rɛkəg,naɪz] (v.) 認出
8 supper ['sʌpɚ] (n.) 晚餐

"Shall we tell them, Mike?" I asked, looking from him to my mother and father.

"Well, we'll need them to promise[1] not to tell anyone," he answered, only half joking.

So we told them all about it, showed them our notes, drawings, maps and photographs. They were very impressed and very complimentary[2], about our hard work.

THINK

- Do you think it was a good idea for the boys to decide to keep the ospreys a secret?
- Why did they tell Don's parents? Was that a good idea?
- Would you have kept it a secret or told someone else?

1 promise [ˈprɑmɪs] (v.) 承諾
2 complimentary [ˌkɑmpləˈmɛntərɪ] (a.) 讚賞的
3 van [væn] (n.) 廂型車
4 roadside [ˈrodˌsaɪd] (n.) 路邊
5 wheel [hwil] (v.) 轉動
6 middle-aged [ˈmɪdḷˌedʒd] (a.) 中年的
7 approach [əˈprotʃ] (v.) 接近
8 expert [ˈɛkspɚt] (n.) 專家
9 glance [glæns] (n.) 一瞥

10 puzzled [ˈpʌzḷd] (a.) 困惑的
11 chain [tʃen] (v.) 用鎖鏈拴住
12 presume [prɪˈzum] (v.) 推測
13 whichever [hwɪtʃˈɛvɚ] (pron.) 無論哪個
14 nod [nɑd] (v.) 點頭
15 marvelous [ˈmɑrvələs] (a.) 了不起的
16 sink [sɪŋk] (v.) 下沉（動詞三態：sink; sank/sunk; sunk/sunken）
17 glare [glɛr] (v.) 怒視
18 concerned [kənˈsɝnd] (a.) 關心的

❺ Mr Roberts

The holidays ended and we went back to school. By now the ospreys had finished building their nest at the top of one of the pine trees on the island in the middle of Big Pool. Of course we still went to watch them every weekend, and a couple of nights after school. Now that the days were getting longer.

One Saturday we were surprised to find a white van[3] parked on the roadside[4] near the track, and as we wheeled[5] our bikes down the track to Redman's Farm we saw a middle-aged[6] man standing looking at us. As we approached[7] he said: "Aha, and here come our two bird experts[8]!"

Mike and I exchanged glances[9] that were both puzzled[10] and worried. When we had chained[11] our bikes to the fence, the man said: "Don and Mike, I presume[12]. Though I have no idea which is which." And he laughed.

We stood silently as he looked from one to the other of us, expecting us to say something.

"Well, whichever[13] of you is Don . . .," here I nodded[14] my head, ". . . I have your father to thank for telling me about your marvelous[15] find."

My face burned red, and my heart sank[16]. Mike glared[17] at me angrily. Why had my stupid father gone and told somebody. The man looked at us, and seemed rather concerned[18] at the reaction he had caused.

"I'm sure you're very busy with your studies," he said. "So please don't worry about me. I'll just wander around and see what I can see. Oh, and it's Mr Roberts, by the way. Pleased to meet you." And then he turned and started to walk around the lakes.

As soon as he was 100 meters away, Mike turned on me: "Did you know about this? Why did your father tell him? Who is he? What does he want?"

"I don't know, Mike," I answered, angrily. "I don't know any more than you do."

The rest of the day was very tense[1]. Mr Roberts appeared from time to time[2] on different sides of the pool. He had binoculars and a camera, and he was watching the ospreys and taking photographs. At about midday he came over to where Mike and I were sitting watching the birds.

"I'm off now," he said. "Thank you very much for your help. And give my best wishes to your father, Don."

"What help?" asked Mike after he'd gone. "We didn't give him any help. I really don't like that man."

"Neither do I," I answered. "Don't worry. I'll ask my dad about him when I get home."

THINK

- How did the boys feel when they met Mr Roberts?
- Who is Mr Roberts? What do you think he wants?

❻ Dad explains

By the time I got home that evening I was really angry. I felt Dad had betrayed[3] our trust by telling someone else about the ospreys. I stormed[4] into the kitchen, where he and my mother were sitting having dinner.

"Dad," I shouted. "What have you done? Who is Mr Roberts? Why did you tell him about the ospreys when we asked you not to?!"

My parents looked at me with puzzled expressions[5]. I wasn't usually aggressive[6].

"Sorry," I said, trying to calm[7] down. "But today a man called Mr Roberts arrived at Redman's Pools, saying you'd told him about us and the ospreys."

My father looked a bit embarrassed[8]. My mother looked worried.

---

1 tense [tɛns] (a.) 緊張的
2 from time to time 不時；偶而
3 betray [bɪˋtre] (v.) 背叛
4 storm [stɔrm] (v.) 橫衝直撞
5 expression [ɪkˋsprɛʃən] (n.) 表情
6 aggressive [əˋgrɛsɪv] (a.) 侵略的
7 calm [kɑm] (v.) 平靜
8 embarrassed [ɪmˋbærəst] (a.) 尷尬的

"He's a business contact[1]," my father started. "We were chatting[2] about things over lunch, and I happened to mention your interest in birds. He said he was a birdwatcher, too, and things went on from there. I'm sorry, I know I shouldn't have told him about the ospreys, but I was so proud of what you and Mike are doing that I'm afraid I said too much."

"But Dad," I went on, "You knew it was really important not to say anything . . ."

"Don't worry, love," said my mother. "I'm sure he's just a birdwatcher like you."

"Well, I hope so," I said bitterly[3], and I walked out of the kitchen and up to my room.

THINK

- Have you ever been angry with your parents? When and why?
- Why is Mike so worried about Mr Roberts knowing about the ospreys?

---

1 contact ['kɑntækt] (n.) 熟人
2 chat [tʃæt] (v.) 聊天；閒談
3 bitterly ['bɪtəlɪ] (adv.) 生氣地；激烈地

❼ Mr Roberts again

Mike and I went to RP all the next day—Sunday—and every evening after that, but there was no white van and no Mr Roberts. Nor the following weekend. But when I was on the bus to school the following Monday I saw the same van parked by the roadside as we went past. I jumped up and rang the bell.

I decided not to go down the main path[1] toward Redman's Farm as we usually did. Instead, I went along another, less-used[2] path which ran behind Castle Hill. This brought me to the trees between Marsh Pool and Big Pool. I also had the advantage[3] of being higher and hidden in the trees, so I could look down onto Big Pool without being seen.

I scanned the scene through my binoculars. There was no sign of Mr Roberts. One of the ospreys was sitting on the nest, probably the female[4], and the other one was sitting on a branch near to the nest eating a fish. Then I saw a flash[5] of blue over to the left. I looked and saw Mr Roberts walking along the side of Big Pool with a large blue plastic[6] bag over his shoulder.

He stopped at the point where the bank was closest to the island and started doing something with the bag. I couldn't see very well because of the bushes and trees, so I moved quietly to find a place where I could see better.

---

1 path [pæθ] (n.) 小徑
2 less-used [lɛsˋjuzd] (a.) 少用的
3 advantage [ədˋvæntɪdʒ] (n.) 優勢
4 female [ˋfimel] (n.) 雌性動物
5 flash [flæʃ] (n.) 閃光
6 plastic [ˋplæstɪk] (a.) 塑膠製的
7 horrified [ˋhɔrəˌfaɪd] (a.) 恐懼的
8 inflatable [ɪnˋfletəbl] (a.) 膨脹的

THINK

- What do you think Mr Roberts is carrying in his bag?

I was horrified[7] by what I saw. Mr Roberts had taken a small inflatable[8] plastic dinghy[9] out of his blue bag, and he was blowing it up with a foot pump[10]. He was going to row over to the ospreys' island!

It took him about ten minutes to fully inflate[11] the boat. Then he placed it in the water, put in his bag and got in. The dinghy was small and there was just enough room for him and his bag. He took out a small plastic paddle[12] and started to row[13] himself across the water to the island.

The male osprey gave a sharp "kew-kew" of warning and flew off its branch, and circled around. The female on the nest looked worried but didn't move. The male flew off and settled on a tree on the other side of the lake, still watching as the small boat got closer to the island.

Mr Roberts maneuvered[14] his boat around to the eastern side of the island. He climbed out onto a small rocky beach. Then he pulled the boat out of the water and made his way towards the four trees. It was quite difficult because the whole island was covered in thick bushes. I watched as he fought his way to the trees, stamping the bushes down as he went.

---

9 dinghy [ˈdɪŋgɪ] (n.) 小艇
10 pump [pʌmp] (n.) 唧筒；打氣筒
11 inflate [ɪnˈflet] (v.) 使膨脹
12 paddle [ˈpædl̩] (n.) 槳
13 row [ro] (v.) 划
14 maneuver [məˈnuvɚ] (v.) 巧妙地操縱

I was boiling[1] with anger inside. What was this man doing? When he got to the trees he looked up to see which one had the nest in it. Next he pushed his way through bushes to the side of the island facing where he had come from, and where I was.

He looked across in my direction, and I held my breath and kept very still, hoping he couldn't see me. Then he went back to the boat and took something out of the blue bag. At first I couldn't see what it was, but I soon realized that it was a long rope. Was he going to climb up the tree?

Then he took the rope back to the nesting tree, and tied one end of it round the base[2] of the tree, pulling it a few times to test that it wouldn't come loose[3]. After that he walked through the bushes again, letting the rope out along the ground as he went, until he reached the water's edge[4] on my side of the island. He covered the rope with grass[5] so it was not visible from where I was, and left the coil[6] dangling[7] at the water's edge.

Then he went back to the plastic boat, put it in the water, got in it and paddled round to where the coil of rope was hanging. He untied[8] the coil, and then rowed slowly back to the land below me, letting the rope out into the water as he went.

---

1 boil [bɔɪl] (v.) 激動
2 base [bes] (n.) 底部
3 loose [lus] (a.) 鬆的
4 edge [ɛdʒ] (n.) 邊緣
5 grass [græs] (n.) 草
6 coil [kɔɪl] (n.) (一)圈
7 dangle [ˈdæŋgl̩] (v.) 懸蕩;吊
8 untie [ʌnˈtaɪ] (v.) 解開

When he got back to the path, he pulled the boat out of the water and tied the end of his rope to the trunk[1] of one of the trees that was leaning[2] over the water. Next he checked from both sides to see that it couldn't be seen by anyone passing by. Finally, he took some luminous[3] yellow sticky tape[4] out of his bag and stuck[5] a small piece on a branch of the tree. Mr Roberts then stood back and admired his work. I looked at his face. There was a smile on it.

He then collected his boat and his blue bag and started to walk very quickly back along the bank of Big Pool towards Redman's Farm. I wondered why he hadn't let the air out of the boat and folded it back in his bag.

Then he walked up to the farm and put the boat into one of the old outhouses[6]. He then shut the door, and locked it with a small padlock[7] which he took out of his pocket. Then he stuck another piece of the yellow tape on the door, and left.

I stayed where I was for a long time, thinking about what I had seen. First there was the rope in the water—what was that for? Maybe to pull himself across the water more quickly than by paddling. And then he left the boat at Redman's Farm to save himself ten minutes or so. And he marked the tree and the door with yellow tape so he knew where to go next time. The more I thought about it, the more it became obvious[8]: he was going to take the ospreys' eggs.

---

1 trunk [trʌŋk] (n.) 樹幹
2 lean [lin] (v.) 傾斜
3 luminous [ˋlumənəs] (a.) 發亮的
4 sticky tape 膠帶
5 stick [stɪk] (v.) 黏貼（動詞三態：stick; stuck; stuck）
6 outhouse [ˋaʊtˌhaʊs] (n.) 附屬建築
7 padlock [ˋpædˌlɑk] (n.) 掛鎖
8 obvious [ˋɑbvɪəs] (a.) 明顯的

As soon as I realized this I felt really angry. How could he?! And then I felt mad[9] at myself. After all, Mike and I had told my dad, who'd told Mr Roberts, so really it was our fault. And if it was our fault we had to make sure that nothing happened to the eggs.

I looked at my watch—it was only ten o'clock, but I decided not to go to school. Instead, I took out my mobile[10] and texted Mike: Meet at RP 5. V UGNT.

THINK

- What would you have done if you were Don?
- What else could he have done?

I walked down to the path and looked at Mr. Roberts' handiwork[11]—the rope and the yellow tape. I was about to pull the tape off and untie the rope, but then I decided to leave them until Mike came and saw what he'd done. Next I walked up to the farm outhouses and looked at the door with its shiny new padlock and yellow tape. I wondered for a moment why he had chosen that particular building, but then I looked in two or three others and saw that they were all full of rubbish[12], so I supposed that it was cleaner than the others.

---

9 mad [mæd] (a.) 發瘋的；生氣的
10 mobile [ˈmobɪl] (a.) 手機
   (= mobile phone)
11 handiwork [ˈhændɪ͵wɝk] (n.) 手工藝品
12 rubbish [ˈrʌbɪʃ] (n.) 垃圾

I had six more hours to wait until Mike arrived, so I sat down and made notes on the ospreys' behavior. At one point I saw the male catch a fish and take it to the female, who was sitting on her precious eggs. She called "pyep, pyep" as he approached. Then she stood up and stretched[1] a little and flapped[2] her wings before eating. The male flew off to his favorite branch on the next tree.

I started thinking. How could anyone want to spoil[3] something so beautiful by taking eggs? And for what, just to sit in glass cases and be looked at occasionally[4]! It seemed ridiculous to me. And what's more, it was illegal. Perhaps we ought to tell the police? I needed to talk to Mike about it.

THINK

- Do you think Don and Mike should tell the police about Mr Roberts?

1 stretch [strɛtʃ] (v.) 展開	6 remove [rɪ`muv] (v.) 拿掉
2 flap [flæp] (v.) 拍打	7 had better 最好……
3 spoil [spɔɪl] (v.) 搞糟	8 evidence [`ɛvədəns] (n.) 證據
4 occasionally [ə`keʒənlɪ] (adv.) 偶爾	9 keep watch 監視
5 initially [ɪ`nɪʃəlɪ] (adv.) 最初地	10 rarely [`rɛrlɪ] (adv.) 鮮少

❽ Mike hears the bad news

Mike arrived shortly after five o'clock. When I told him what had happened, his face grew more and more worried. We walked to the outhouse first, and then to the tree where the rope was tied. I pulled it out of the water to show him.

"What do you think we should do?" he asked.

"I'm not sure," I replied. "Initially[5] I just wanted to cut the rope, remove[6] the padlock and make a big hole in the boat . . . but then I thought I'd better[7] wait for you and talk it over."

"Thanks," said Mike. "I think it's best if we catch him doing something. We should take some photographs. It's important that we have evidence[8]; then we call the police. They'll know what to do."

"That's a good idea," I answered, "But it means we'll have to keep watch[9]. He obviously came in the morning because he knows we're at school. Which means he won't come in the afternoons or at weekends because that's when we might be here. Also early morning is a time when other people rarely[10] come here."

"Yes, that's probably right," said Mike. "What time did you get here this morning?"

"Well, let's see . . . I got the quarter[1] to eight bus from Saltley to get to school by 8.30, so I suppose it gets here at about 8 o'clock, doesn't it?" I answered.

> **THINK**
>
> - Why is it important for the boys to "have evidence" of what Mr Roberts is doing?

"It's strange he never thought about us seeing his van from the bus," said Mike. "He mustn't be local or he would have known you go past, or else he thinks we both go to my school and don't come this way. I wonder where he's from."

"I can ask Dad," I answered. "He'll know."

"Good idea. See what you can find out," replied Mike. "But don't blame[2] your father. It's our fault for telling him in the first place[3]."

"Yeah, I know," I said. "And it's up to us[4] to make sure Mr Roberts' plans don't work, so that we can make up[5] for our mistake."

"Agreed," said Mike. "Right now, I think we should take some photographs of the rope, the yellow markers, the outhouse door and padlock so we have some evidence to back us up[6]. But I think we should leave everything as it is, and keep watch."

"OK, Mike," I said. "But it means we'll have to be here during the day while he's setting up his equipment[7]. He's obviously going to need something to get up to the nest. It's quite a climb—a good[8] 12 meters high."

"That's right," Mike answered. "I'll come tomorrow, and then we can take it in turns missing school. We'll keep in touch by texting[9] each other during the day. And then we'll meet at 5 after school."

"Right," I agreed. "Now let's get those photos."

THINK

- Do you think the boys are doing the right thing?

---

1 quarter [`kwɔrtɚ] (n.) 一刻鐘
2 blame [blem] (v.) 責備
3 in the first place 一開始
4 up to sb 決定於某人
5 make up 彌補
6 back up 支持
7 equipment [ɪ`kwɪpmənt] (n.) 裝備
8 a good 至少
9 text [tɛkst] (v.) 發簡訊

❾ More about Mr Roberts

That evening, while we were watching TV, I asked my father what he knew about Mr Roberts.

"Well, not a lot, really, Don," he answered. "He works for a company called Johnson Electricals[1] that my company does some business with. He's their Sales Manager, and I met him to discuss a business deal[2] to buy some components[3] we need."

"Where's he from?" I asked.

"The company's based[4] in Leicester," answered my dad. "But I don't know if he lives there."

"Is that all you know?" I asked, disappointed[5].

"Well, let's think," he said. "When I had lunch with him we talked about . . . well, apart from the birds, we talked about . . . er, football, a bit of politics[6], probably something about work in our line[7] of business . . . I mean just general chat over lunch."

"Is there any way you can find out where he lives?" I asked.

"Well, not really," my dad said. "It's not the sort[8] of thing you can do, is it? I mean, ring up a business acquaintance[9] and ask: 'Where do you live?' Anyway, why are you so interested in Mr Roberts all of a sudden[10]?"

1　electricals [ɪˈlɛktrɪklz] (n.) 電子公司
2　deal [dil] (n.) 交易
3　component [kəmˈponənt] (n.) 零件
4　base [bes] (v.) 以……為基地
5　disappoint [ˌdɪsəˈpɔɪnt] (v.) 使失望
6　politics [ˈpɑlətɪks] (n.) 政治
7　line [laɪn] (n.) 行業
8　sort [sɔrt] (n.) 種類
9　acquaintance [əˈkwentəns] (n.) 認識的人
10　all of a sudden 突然地

 "Oh, nothing important," I answered, not wanting to give away[1] anything about what had happened that morning. "Just see if you can think of a way of finding out, will you?"

I left the room, with my father watching TV with a puzzled expression on his face. In my bedroom I texted Mike: no info re R.

> **THINK**
>
> - Why do you think **Don** doesn't want to tell his father about what **Mr Roberts** has been doing?

The next two days at RP were uneventful[2] for Mike first, and me second. Mr Roberts didn't come on either day, so we just met after school and watched the ospreys and made notes and came home on the bus.

But that second night my father came home from work with some news.

"I spoke to your friend Mr Roberts today, Don," he started, with a smile over dinner.

"And . . .?" I asked.

"He rang me up[3] to talk about the contract[4]," he went on. "And I asked him whether he could come over to sign details tomorrow. He said it was no problem because he lives in Rittington, which is halfway between Leicester and here."

"That's great, Dad," I said, "Thanks very much. Oh . . . one more thing. Do you happen to know his name?"

"Yes, it's Steve," he answered. "But I still don't understand why you want . . ."

But I was out of the room by then, taking the telephone directory[5] from the hall table up to my room.

And a few minutes later I found what I was looking for:

| Roberts Mr S | 24 Golding Lane, Rittington | 43879122 |

---

1 give away 洩露
2 uneventful [ˌʌnɪˈvɛntfəl]
   (a.) 平靜無事的
3 ring up 打電話

4 contract [ˈkɑntrækt] (n.) 合約；合同
5 directory [dəˈrɛktərɪ] (n.) 姓名住址簿；號碼簿

I wrote it down on my note[1] pad[2], and then texted Mike: R lives Rittington.

And soon there was a reply[3]: GR8.

And then I remembered what my father had said and I ran downstairs again.

"Dad," I started, "Did you say you were meeting Mr Roberts tomorrow?"

"Yes," he answered. "Why?"

"When is your meeting?" I asked him.

"In the afternoon," he said. "He said he was busy in the morning somewhere else in the area."

"Thanks, Dad," I said. And I started to leave the room.

"Don," my dad said, "What is all this interest in Steve Roberts all of a sudden?"

"Oh, nothing," I replied. "But whatever you do, don't mention the ospreys, Mike and me, or my questions. Please!"

"Don't worry," he said laughing. "I know I've put my foot in it[4] once. I won't say a word."

Back in my room I texted Mike: Think R at RP 2moro. Me 2.

I had decided that I would go too, although it was Mike's turn to be on duty[5]. He might need some help, and anyway I wanted to see what would happen next.

Mike texted back: CU.

---

1 note [not] (n.) 便條
2 pad [pæd] (n.) 便條紙簿
3 reply [rɪˋplaɪ] (n.) 回覆
4 put one's foot in it 搞砸事情
5 on duty 值班
6 creep [krip] (v.) 躡手躡足地走（動詞三態：creep; crept/creeped; crept/creeped）
7 pull up 使停下來
8 registration number 汽車牌照號碼
9 make [mek] (n.) 品牌；樣式

❶⓪ At Redman's Pools

So very early on Thursday morning I crept[6] out of the house and got the early bus. At 6.30 I got off at the stop nearest to Redman's Pools and walked over to the path. Just then the white van pulled up[7] and parked in its usual place. I hid behind the trees as Mr Roberts got out and took his blue bag out of the back, then locked up and set off down the path to Redman's Farm.

I texted Mike: RU at RP? Then I wrote down the registration number[8] (S 471 AJB) and make[9] of the van in my notebook.

My phone vibrated: at Castle Hill read the message.

I texted back: R here 2. CU 5 mins. And I went to the place where I always met Mike.

"Hi. Can you see him?" I asked as I sat down.

"Hi, Don," Mike replied. "Yes, he's at Redman's Farm."

Mike was looking at Mr Roberts through his binoculars. I took mine out and looked for the ospreys. The male was sitting in a tree on the other side of the lake, and the female was sitting on the nest.

"He's getting the boat out," said Mike.

I turned my binoculars to watch. Steve Roberts stood the boat against the wall, and locked the door. Then he looked at his watch and walked back up the track to the road and disappeared[1] from sight[2], leaving the boat where it was and his blue bag next to it.

> **THINK**
> - Where has Mr Roberts gone?

"Strange," I said.

"Perhaps he's left something in his van," Mike guessed.

But our answer soon came, when Mr Roberts reappeared with a younger man.

"I wonder who this is", I said.

"An accomplice[3], obviously," Mike said.

We watched in silence[4] as the two men walked to the farm. Mr Roberts picked up the boat and the younger man took the blue bag. Then they walked in our direction down the path.

Mr Roberts pointed out the birds and the nest to the young man. They stopped when they got to the tree with the yellow marker[5] tape. Mr Roberts opened the blue bag and took out a new rope. He tied it onto a ring on the front of the boat, and tied the other end to the tree. After that the two men talked. Mr Roberts was obviously explaining what they were going to do.

"What are they doing?" I whispered to Mike.

"Roberts is showing him how they're going to get over to the island," he replied. "It'll be interesting to see how they do it, because they can't both get into that little boat."

We didn't have long to wait. Mr Roberts got into the boat, took his blue bag from the young man, sat down, reached[6] for the underwater rope, and very quickly and easily pulled himself over to the island.

"That was faster than with the paddle!" I exclaimed.

When he was standing on the island, he gave a thumbs-up[7] to the young man, who pulled the boat back with the new rope attached[8] to the ring. Then he got in, untied the new rope from the tree, and pulled himself over to the island to join Mr Roberts. He got out and they pulled the boat up onto the land together.

"Very clever," said Mike.

"Clever and fast," I replied. "They want to be out of here quickly."

Then the two men walked to the ospreys' tree and stood at the base talking and looking up. Then the young man sat down, and did something. We couldn't see what he was doing because of the bushes.

---

1 disappear [ˌdɪsəˈpɪr] (v.) 消失
2 sight [saɪt] (n.) 視線
3 accomplice [əˈkɑmplɪs] (n.)
   共犯；幫兇
4 silence [ˈsaɪləns] (n.) 沉默
5 marker [ˈmɑrkɚ] (n.) 做記號的人或物
6 reach [ritʃ] (v.) 伸出（手）
7 thumbs-up [ˌθʌmzˈʌp] (n.) 翹大拇指
8 attach [əˈtætʃ] (v.) 繫上

When he stood up, he was wearing a yellow safety helmet[1] with a lamp in the front—the kind that miners[2] and cavers[3] wear. He was holding a special sort of belt which was attached to his waist; he put this round the trunk of the next tree, not the ospreys' one. And then he raised his arms, leaned back, and jumped up with his feet on either side of the tree . . . and, to our amazement, he stayed there.

He then climbed up to about 2 meters off the ground, by alternately[4] moving the belt up, and jumping up with his feet.

"Hey," said Mike, "he must have special climbing spikes[5] on his shoes so that he can hold on."

"Yes, and I bet[6] he's a professional[7] climber," I replied. "Roberts knew he couldn't climb the tree himself, so he's hired[8] a professional."

The young climber came down the trunk, and the two men talked some more. Then the young man disappeared from view to take off his gear[9], after which the two of them went back to the boat. Mr Roberts tied the boat rope onto a small tree near the water, and the climber got into the boat and started to pull himself back to the land.

"Quick!" said Mike. "Get some photos!"

We were so interested in the two men that we'd forgotten to collect more photographic[10] evidence. We took out our cameras and took some photos as both men pulled themselves back to the land.

As they started to walk back towards the farm, Mike said: "Stay here." He ran away so quickly I didn't have time to ask what he was going to do.

I stayed where I was and took some more photos with the zoom[1], as the men put their equipment back into the outhouse and Mr Roberts locked the door. Then they walked off, deep in conversation.

About fifteen minutes later I heard Mike coming back through the trees.

"What was all that about?" I asked as he sat down, out of breath[2].

"I thought I'd go and see if I could get some more information," he said.

"And?" I asked.

"I hid behind a tree near their cars and listened to what they were saying," he replied. "They're meeting tomorrow night at ten o'clock."

"Tomorrow night," I repeated. "After dark."

"Yes, well it's too obvious[3] in the day, isn't it?" Mike said. "I mean someone could come and see them, or we could be around, but after dark they think there'll be no one around. Oh, and I also got the number and make of the climber's car."

"Well done, Sherlock Holmes[4]!" I joked. But I was really impressed at my friend's quick thinking.

"Elementary[5], my dear Watson!" he joked back.

THINK

- Who are Sherlock Holmes and Dr Watson? Why do the boys refer to them?

⓫ Plans for the next night

"So what shall we do?" asked Mike as we sat in my bedroom later that afternoon.

"Well, my first idea was to stop them before they start," I said. "I mean, we could destroy[6] the boat and cut the ropes."

"Yeah, that was my first thought, too," said Mike.

"But then I started to think more long term[7]," I said.

"What do you mean?" Mike asked.

"Well, think about it," I began. "I'm absolutely[8] certain that this is not the only egg that Steve Roberts has stolen in his life. And I'm sure he'll steal more in the future. He's a criminal[9], Mike. He might keep one egg for his own collection and sell the others for a large sum[10] of money to other collectors. We need to stop him for ever, not just for now. So if we just destroy his equipment it will save these ospreys' chicks[11], which is good, but if he's caught with the eggs, then he'll be put in prison or be fined[12], or both, and his egg collection will be taken away and put in a museum. One thing's for sure: it'll stop him for good."

---

1 zoom [zum] (n.) 變焦鏡頭
2 out of breath 喘不過氣來
3 obvious [ˈɑbvɪəs] (a.) 明顯的
4 Sherlock Holmes [ˈʃɜlɑk homz]
  福爾摩斯（偵探小說的主人翁）
5 elementary [ˌɛləˈmɛntərɪ] (a.)
  初級的

6 destroy [dɪˈstrɔɪ] (v.) 破壞
7 long term 長期
8 absolutely [ˈæbsəˌlutlɪ] (adv.) 絕對地
9 criminal [ˈkrɪmənl̩] (n.) 罪犯
10 sum [sʌm] (n.) 總數
11 chick [tʃɪk] (n.) 小鳥；雛鳥
12 fine [faɪn] (v.) 罰款

"That's very good thinking, Don," said Mike. "So have you got any ideas about what we should do?"

"Well, I don't think we should hand it over[1] to the police. Because if they turn up[2] in cars with lights and sirens[3], they're going to frighten Roberts and the climber off before they even start. And that will be no good."

"Agreed," said Mike. "But on the other hand[4] we can't do it all by ourselves, can we?"

"No, I don't think we can," I said, "But what we can do is to set it all up[5] ourselves so that when the police come, they get the whole picture[6] very clearly."

"I can see you've got some sort of[7] an idea in your head, Don," said Mike, laughing, "So let's hear it."

"OK," I said. "Has your dad still got those spotlights[8] and car batteries which he used when you had that party in your garden last winter?"

"Yeah," Mike answered. "They're in the garage. I saw them a few days ago, in fact, and wondered if he'd ever use them again."

"Right," I said, "We take them to RP and set them up tomorrow morning so that they shine onto the ospreys' tree on the island."

"They're heavy, you know," said Mike. "How will we get them there?"

"We can manage on our bikes—four lights and four batteries shouldn't be too much to manage—two for you, two for me," I answered. "When you get home, charge[9] the batteries, will you, so that there's plenty of power in them."

"Yes, sir!" said Mike, and saluted[10] like a soldier[11]. I smiled.

"So, first we set up the lights," I went on. "Then tomorrow night we wait for Roberts and his friend to go onto the island. When the climber goes up the tree and gets the eggs, we turn on the lights, take photographs and the police can arrest[12] them."

"OK," said Mike. "Good plan. Just one question—where do the police come from?"

"Well, we'll go and see old Sergeant[13] Keddle at the village police station tomorrow and explain everything to him," I said. "We can ask him to come along to RP at about 9 o'clock and sit and wait with us. I'm sure he'll want to help out."

"But what if he wants to take over[14] and do it another way? You know, call in other police officers to help out?" asked Mike.

---

1 hand over 交出
2 turn up 出現
3 siren ['saɪrən] (n.) 警報器
4 on the other hand 就另一方面來說
5 set up 豎立；架起；計畫
6 get the whole picture 掌握整個狀況
7 sort of 有點兒

8 spotlight ['spɑk,laɪt] (n.) 聚光燈
9 charge [tʃɑrdʒ] (v.) 充電
10 salute [sə'lut] (v.) 行禮
11 soldier ['soldʒɚ] (n.) 士兵；軍人
12 arrest [ə'rɛst] (v.) 逮捕
13 sergeant ['sɑrdʒənt] (n.) 警官
14 take over 接管

"I don't think he will," I replied. "We both know what he's like. We've known him all our lives. He's very proud and if we tell him it will be good publicity for him, and he might get promotion, he'll do it our way, I'm sure. We'll have to get some torches[1] and batteries for us to use, too," I said. "I've got that really powerful one. And you've got a good one, too. Oh, and I'll borrow my dad's infra[2]-red night sights[3] so we can see exactly what they're doing."

"And we have to make sure they can't go anywhere very far if they try to run away," said Mike. "Once they're on their way over to the island, I can run round the back of Castle Hill to the road, like I did this morning, and puncture[4] the tires on their vehicles[5] so that they can't go anywhere. Then I'll come straight back. It'll only take me about 10 minutes."

"That's a good idea, Mike," I said. "Yes, it's best if you do it because you're much faster than I am. So remember to bring a very sharp knife that can cut through tire rubber[6] with you."

THINK

- Do you think it's a good idea to tell the village policeman? Why/why not?
- What do you think of the boys' plans? Do you think they will work?

---

1 torch [tɔrtʃ] (n.)〔英〕手電筒
2 infra- [ˈɪnfrə] (pref.) 在下
3 sights [saɪts] (n.)〔複〕瞄準器
4 puncture [ˈpʌŋktʃɚ] (v.) 刺；刺穿
5 vehicle [ˈviːɪkl] (n.) 車輛
6 rubber [ˈrʌbɚ] (n.) 橡膠

7 blacken [ˈblækən] (v.) 塗黑；變黑
8 blond [blɑnd] (a.) 金黃色的
9 as well 也
10 wooly [ˈwʊlɪ] (a.) 羊毛製的 (= woolly)
11 empty [ˈɛmptɪ] (a.) 空的
12 hatch [hætʃ] (v.) 孵化

"My dad has just the thing in his toolbox. I'll get that." Mike said. "Now, is there anything else we need to think about?"

"Clothes," I answered. "We need to wear black clothes with nothing shiny on them, and we should probably blacken[7] our faces a bit, too, but some mud from the lake should be good enough for that. And you'll need a hat to cover your blond[8] hair as well[9]!"

"Right," Mike said. "I've got a woolly[10] winter hat. It's dark blue."

"And we'll have to think about school," I said.

"Why don't you come straight over to my house?" said Mike. "My mum and dad leave earlier than me, so the place will be empty[11] all day."

"Good idea," I said. "And the best thing would be if you went home on my bike now, so that it's ready at your house for me to use in the morning to take the spotlights and batteries out to RP."

"OK," agreed Mike. "Now if that's everything, I'll go now and get ready."

"There is one thing I've just thought about," I said. "How are we going to stay out so late without our parents worrying about where we are?"

"Easy," said Mike. "You tell your parents you're going to stay over at my house for the night, and I'll tell my parents I'm going to stay with you. We can say we're going to RP straight after school because the ospreys are getting ready for the eggs to hatch[12], and that we want to go back again early on Saturday morning for the same reason. They should believe us."

"Fine," I said. "Let's try that and hope that they don't meet in the village or telephone each other!!"

We both laughed. Then Mike left and cycled[1] home on my bike.

I started getting my backpack[2] ready for the next night. I even remembered to put two apples and some chocolate in there as well. It was going to be a long day and night!

1 cycle ['saɪkl̩] (v.) 騎腳踏車
2 backpack ['bæk,pæk] (n.)（登山、遠足用的）背包
3 suspicious [sə'spɪʃəs] (a.) 猜疑的
4 casually ['kæʒjuəlɪ] (adv.) 若無其事地

⓵⓶ A busy morning

   My alarm clock rang at six o'clock on Friday morning, and I started to get ready. I had to put on my school uniform so my parents wouldn't get suspicious[3]. It's quite difficult to act normal when you have such an important day ahead, and you have to keep it secret. Luckily, my parents are always very sleepy when they get up in the morning and they don't really notice anything.

   Just as I was walking out of the door I said, as casually[4] as I could: "Oh, by the way, I think I forgot to say last night—I'm going to sleep over at Mike's tonight because we want to stay at RP as late as possible this evening. And we'll be going back there very early tomorrow morning, too. So, I'll see you tomorrow evening. Bye." And I walked out of the door before they could say anything.

   I walked slowly down to the center of the village, and called in at the newspaper shop to buy a bottle of water to take out to RP. It would be thirsty work. Then I walked round to Mike's house.

   It was just after a quarter to eight. Normally I would be on the bus at this time.

As I got closer to Mike's house, I saw his father's car turning out of the drive[1] into the road.

I hid behind a tree and watched as the car went past to see whether his mother and father were both inside. They were.

Once the car had turned the corner, I walked quickly along to Mike's house, rang the bell and he let me in.

"How did it go this morning?" he asked.

"Oh, fine. I've got all the things we need in here. I just saw your mum and dad leaving. Did they suspect[2] anything?"

THINK

- Don lies to his parents. How do you think he feels?
- Have you ever lied to your parents? How did you feel?

1 drive [draɪv] (n.) 車道
2 suspect [səˋspɛkt] (v.) 懷疑；察覺
3 load [lod] (v.) 裝載
4 disconnect [ˌdɪskəˋnɛkt] (v.) 切斷 （電源）
5 charger [ˋtʃɑrdʒɚ] (n.) 充電器
6 gloomy [ˋglumɪ] (a.) 陰暗的
7 fix [fɪks] (v.) 使固定
8 the best part of an hour 將近一個鐘頭
9 lookout [ˋlukˋaut] (n.) 守望；監視
10 unload [ʌnˋlod] (v.) 卸載

"Not a thing!" he replied. "Now what'll we do first?"

"I have to get out of my school uniform. I brought a change of clothes with me," I said. "And I'd prefer to leave my school bag here, too, if that's alright with you."

"Of course," Mike answered and led the way up to his room.

I got changed quickly and hid my bag and school clothes under his bed. "Now, let's go and load[3] up the bikes and get out to RP."

We went into the garage, and he disconnected[4] the battery charger[5]. We put the batteries in the lamps and checked that they were working. They were very powerful in the gloomy[6] garage.

"I fixed[7] a large plastic fruit box to the back of each bike last night," Mike said, "So that we can carry things more easily."

I looked at his work. "That was a good idea," I said.

We loaded two batteries and two lamps into each basket and pushed the bikes out into the drive. I put my backpack on while Mike locked up the house. Then we set off.

It was hard work cycling as the lights and batteries were heavy, and it took us the best part of an hour[8] to get there instead of our usual half an hour. We got off our bikes and wheeled them round the back path behind Castle Hill until we got to what had become our lookout[9] point.

First we unloaded[10] the batteries and lamps; then we hid the bikes behind some bushes.

Then we relaxed and watched the ospreys for a while. Though we were both nervous at the thought of what was going to happen later.

> **THINK**
>
> - Think of a time when you felt nervous before an event.
>   Try and describe your feelings to a partner.
> - Why were you nervous?

"Strange, isn't it?" I said. "These birds have no idea what's going on, have they?"

We both laughed.

"Come on, then," Mike said. "Let's get started. I suggest we go and look for the best places to put the lamps before we carry them all the way down here."

So we walked down to the lakeside and discussed where we should put them. We needed to find places that would give us the best direct light onto the island, and yet at the same time wouldn't be seen by Roberts or the climber. In the end we chose four places spread[1] along either side of the tree where Roberts had tied the rope.

After that we went back to get the first two batteries. We had just positioned[2] the first lamp and were looking for a place for the second one, when we turned a corner and walked straight into Mr Roberts. He looked as shocked as we felt, but then he quickly changed his expression to a broad[3] smile.

"Hello, boys," he said. "How nice to see you again. I was just passing by on my way to work and I thought I'd drop in[4] and see how our feathered friends are getting on[5]."

"Good morning, Mr Roberts," I managed to say.

"Shouldn't you be at school on a Friday morning?" he asked looking from one of us to the other.

"Well . . . er . . ." I tried.

"Actually, we've got the day off," lied Mike. "It's a special school holiday."

"I see," he said. "And what on earth[6] are you doing with that car battery?"

"Um . . . we've . . . er . . . we're . . . going to do some sound recordings tomorrow," I lied. "So we brought the battery down today." The lying was getting easier.

"You could come and watch if you're interested."

"Er . . . well, I'm a bit busy tomorrow, I'm afraid," Mr Roberts said. "So thanks, but I can't."

"Pity," I said. "It'll be great fun."

"I'm sure it will be," he answered. "Erm . . . are you going to be staying here long today?"

"Not really," I answered. "Probably another couple of hours, and then we'll be off. We're getting the tape recorder[7] from a friend so we have to go and collect it this afternoon."

---

1 spread [sprɛd] (v.) 散布
2 position [pəˋzɪʃən] (v.) 安置；放置
3 broad [brɔd] (a.) 寬闊的
4 drop in 順道來訪
5 get on 進展
6 on earth 究竟
7 tape recorder 錄音機

"Oh, good . . . er . . . right," he said. "Well, I must be going[1]. Nice to see you again . . . and good luck with the recordings."

"Thank you, Mr Roberts," Mike said as he walked away down the path.

Mike and I stood there for a good few minutes until he had walked down the path to the road and we heard the distant[2] noise of his van starting and driving quickly away.

> ## THINK
>
>
>
> - How did Mike and Don feel when they met Mr Roberts unexpectedly?
> - Have you ever had an unpleasant surprise? When? How did you feel and what did you do?

"Wow!" said Mike. "That was close!"

"Yes," I said. "Imagine if we were putting the lamps up when he came along. How would we have explained that?"

"Well, you were brilliant[3]!" he said. "I didn't know you could lie so well. You looked so serious, I nearly believed you. Sound recordings indeed[4]! How did you think of that?"

We laughed.

"I've no idea," I answered. "But I'm very glad I thought of it! Now let's get this done. We've wasted enough time already."

---

1 be going 告辭
2 distant [ˈdɪstənt] (a.) 遠的
3 brilliant [ˈbrɪljənt] (a.) 厲害的
4 indeed [ɪnˈdid] (adv.) 確實地

5 set to 開始認真幹活
6 completely [kəmˈplitlɪ] (adv.) 完全地
7 invisible [ɪnˈvɪzəbl] (a.) 看不到的
8 chance [tʃæns] (v.) 冒……險

"Yes," said Mike as I picked up the battery. "But why do you suppose he came here this morning?"

"Probably just to check that everything was ready for tonight," I replied.

"I guess so," he said. And we set to[5] work.

For the next hour we set up all four batteries and lamps, and tested them. The lamps were so bright you could even see them in the sunshine. Then we checked they were completely[6] invisible[7] from the path.

"Just one point," Mike said as we finished off. "How will we find them in the dark? Because we won't be able to use our torches or they'll see us too soon. The same goes for the night sights. We need to be hidden before we can chance[8] using them. They'll see the red light."

"You're right," I said. And I thought for a moment. "I know— let's count[9] the number of steps from our lookout to the lamps. I'll switch the two on the right on[10] and you switch the two on the left on."

And that's what we did. We went back up to the lookout and carefully counted our steps to the lamps. Mine were fifteen and twenty paces[11] away from the lookout, and Mike's were eighteen and twenty-two.

"And we'll have to make sure we switch them on at the same time. But we can synchronize[12] our watches," said Mike. "We can decide all that this evening when we see how things are going."

I looked at my watch. "Agreed," I said. "Now it's eleven o'clock. Let's cycle back to Saltley and go and talk to Sergeant Keddle."

---

9 count [kaʊnt] (v.) 計算
10 switch on 打開（電源）
11 pace [pes] (n.) 一步
12 synchronize [ˈsɪŋkrənaɪz] (v.) 使同步

❶❸ Talking to the policeman

Like many village police stations in England, the building was Sergeant Keddle's house, too. The front room was his office. We rang and waited.

"Hello, boys," said the old policeman when he opened the door. "What can I do for you?"

"We'd like to talk to you, please, Sergeant Keddle," I said.

"Right, boys. Come in, then," he answered, and showed us into his office.

We sat on two chairs in front of his desk while he went and sat behind it.

"So, what's the problem?" he asked.

And we told him everything we knew. We showed him our records, maps, photographs. And then we told him of our plan for the evening.

He stood up and walked up and down in front of the window for a minute or so, then he turned round and looked at us both.

"It's very irregular[1], you know," he said. "And if anything goes wrong we could all be in trouble[2], especially me!"

---

1 irregular [ɪˈrɛgjələ] (a.) 非正規的
2 in trouble 惹上麻煩

"But, Sergeant Keddle," Mike said. "We've got everything perfectly planned and ready. Nothing will go wrong, and when we catch[1] Roberts you'll get nothing but praise[2] for your good work."

"Please, Sergeant Keddle," I added. "Catch this man and get him convicted[3] so he can't steal any more eggs."

He thought for a while longer, and then suddenly said: "Right, boys. Let's do it."

THINK

- Have you ever spoken to a policeman about something serious? When and why?
- How does the policeman feel about their plan at first?
- Why do you think he agrees to do what they suggest?

"Thank you, Sergeant Keddle," we both said together, very relieved[4].

"Let's go over[5] all the arrangements[6]," he said, "But first, give me the numbers of the two vehicles so that I can have them checked."

He phoned up[7] the County[8] Police Headquarters[9] and asked them to call him back with details. We sat and discussed everything: where we were going to meet, that we would have to be quiet and that we shouldn't put the lights on until the right moment. We asked Sergeant Keddle to come in his own car rather than[10] the police car and told him where to park.

While we were talking, the information came through[11] about the cars. As expected the white van belonged to Steve Roberts, and we found out the name of the climber: Bill Henderson from Leicester.

"That's good," said the policemen. "We know exactly who they are and where they're from. That gives us a big advantage."

We talked some more, and went over everything one last time. Then we arranged to meet Sergeant Keddle at nine o'clock that evening and we left. Mike and I cycled back to his house and had something to eat.

"He was very good, wasn't he?" Mike said as we ate some sandwiches.

"Yes," I agreed. "He was so business-like[12] going over the maps and the plans, and noting everything down. I was surprised, really—I didn't really think he was so efficient[13]."

"Well, let's hope he's just as good tonight," said Mike.

---

1 catch [kætʃ] (v.) 抓住
2 praise [prez] (n.) (v.) 稱讚
3 convict [kənˋvɪkt] (v.) 判罪
4 relieve [rɪˋliv] (v.) 使放心
5 go over 察看；重溫
6 arrangement [əˋrendʒmənt] (n.) 安排
7 phone up 打電話

8 county [ˋkauntɪ] (a.) 郡的
9 headquarters [ˋhɛdˋkwɔrtɚz] (n.)〔複〕總局
10 rather than 而不是……
11 come through 透過電話或電郵傳來
12 business-like [ˋbɪznɪsˏlaɪk] (a.) 有效率的；有條理的
13 efficient [ɪˋfɪʃənt] (a.) 效率高的

❶❹ Back to Redman's Pools

At 4 o'clock we got back on our bikes and cycled out to RP for the second time that day. We didn't really need to go so early, but we couldn't risk being in Saltley when our parents came home because of what we'd told them. We cycled slowly. We didn't say very much as we were both thinking about the evening ahead[1].

When we arrived we were pleased to see that neither Roberts' nor Henderson's cars were parked by the path to Redman's Farm. One less problem for us to face. We went in by the back route[2] and hid our bicycles well out of the way.

We went into our lookout and started to check all our equipment. After we were satisfied that everything was ready, we went down to the edge of the lake. We watched the ospreys for a while. The male made some beautiful circuits[3] of the lake and then dived in to catch a large fish, which it took up to the nest and gave to the female, before flying away towards Marsh Pool. We knew from past observations[4] that he sometimes rested on a dead oak[5] tree there. The female stood up and shook herself, stretched her wings and flapped them a few times. Then she started eating.

---

1 ahead [ə'hɛd] (adv.) 將來
2 route [rut] (n.) 路線
3 circuit [ˋsɝkɪt] (n.) 繞行
4 observation [͵ɑbzɝˋveʃən] (n.) 觀察

We practiced walking to the lamps, counting out our steps as we went. We did it with our eyes open at first, but then Mike suggested trying with our eyes closed so that we knew what it would be like in the dark.

It wasn't so easy! We had to remember where the path turned so as not to end up in the lake or in the bushes on the other side.

We decided to go for a walk right round all three lakes to kill some time[6] and try to relax a little. We didn't talk much, except to point out birds and comment[7] on what we saw. We both realized[8] that this was the most serious thing we had ever been involved[9] in.

It was a pleasant[10] evening. There was a light breeze[11] blowing, and we enjoyed the colors in the sky as the sun went down. By eight o'clock we were back in the lookout.

"Do you want an apple, Mike?" I asked, starting to eat mine.

"Thanks," he said, taking it. We ate in silence.

"It's time we got ready," said Mike. "Let's get some mud on our faces so we're camouflaged[12]."

We went down to the lake and scooped[13] up some mud from the bottom.

"You put some on my face and I'll put some on yours," I said.

Once we were ready, Mike went to get Sergeant Keddle.

---

5 oak [ok] (n.) 橡樹
6 kill time 消磨時間
7 comment [ˋkɑmɛnt] (v.) 評論
8 realize [ˋrɪəˌlaɪz] (v.) 了解到
9 involved [ɪnˋvɑlvd] (a.) 牽扯在內的
10 pleasant [ˋplɛznt] (a.) 宜人的
11 breeze [briz] (n.) 微風
12 camouflage [ˋkæməˌflɑʒ] (v.) 偽裝
13 scoop [skup] (v.) 用勺舀

I was left alone with the darkening view of the lake, and my own thoughts. I checked everything I needed once again. I changed my daytime binoculars for my father's infra-red night sights, and practiced using them. I watched the female osprey sitting on her eggs at the top of the pine tree. I thought somehow that this was the end of one time, and the beginning of another. Things would be different for all of us after this evening—for the birds, for Mike and me, for Mr Roberts and Bill Henderson, and for Sergeant Keddle.

THINK

- Why do the boys put mud on their faces? How do you think it feels?
- Why does Don think: "Things would be different for all of us"? Explain what he means.

①⑤ Night action

Soon I heard soft noises behind me, followed by Mike whispering "Don—it's us".

It was Mike and Sergeant Keddle. We exchanged greetings and I briefly shone a small torch around so that the policeman could see where he was. Then we started to explain things to the Sergeant. He was very quick at picking things up[1].

"Right, boys," he said, "It's nine thirty-five. If their ten o'clock arrangement is on[2], we should start watching over by the track they'll use in half an hour. I've brought some night sights of my own—I ordered them from County HQ after you left this afternoon. So I can see the lie of the land[3] pretty well now. This is a very good lookout post[4], boys. Well done."

"Would you like some chocolate?" I asked.

They wanted some, and we ate and enjoyed it in silence.

All of a sudden the darkness was split[5] by a terrible shriek[6].

"Goodness me!" said the policeman. "What on earth was that?"

Mike and I hid our laughter.

---

1 pick things up 理解狀況
2 on [ɑn] (a.) 進行中的
3 the lie of the land 地形；情勢
4 post [post] (n.) 哨所
5 split [splɪt] (v.) 劃開（動詞三態：split; split; split）
6 shriek [ʃrik] (n.) 尖叫聲

"Don't worry," I said. "It's just a barn owl[1]. They nest over in Redman's Farm."

"Yes," said Mike, "But it might mean they've been disturbed by people arriving."

"Quite right, young man," said the Sergeant. "Good point[2]."

> ## THINK
>
> - Have you ever been out in the countryside at night? What was it like? What did you see and hear?
> - What is it like using a torch in the dark? How well can you see?

Both Sergeant Keddle and I focused[3] our night sights on the farm. At first I could see nothing, but then I picked up the occasional flash of light of a torch being flicked[4] on and off[5].

"Did you see that, Sergeant?" I asked.

"I did indeed, Don," he replied.

"What?" asked Mike, who was feeling left out[6].

"There are people—Roberts and Henderson, I suppose—walking around the farm buildings," said the Sergeant.

"Absolutely[7]," I said, "And here they come with the plastic boat. Time for you to go and do their tires, Mike."

---

1 barn owl [barn aʊl] 倉鴞
2 good point 重點
3 focus [ˈfokəs] (v.) 聚焦
4 flick [flɪk] (v.) 突然一動
5 on and off 斷斷續續地
6 left out 被冷落的
7 absolutely [ˈæbsə‚lutlɪ] (adv.) 絕對地

"OK," he said. "Back in ten minutes."

"Where's he going?" asked Sergeant Keedle .

"We decided we would make sure they couldn't get far if they tried to make a run for it[1]," I explained. "So he's going to puncture their tires."

"Good thinking," said the Sergeant. "Very good."

Mike was soon back. "Mission[2] accomplished[3]," he whispered[4].

I handed the night sights over to Mike, because I didn't want him to feel left out. He watched and commented very quietly. "They're down at Big Pool now. Roberts is carrying the boat, and Henderson has got a bag with things in it. They're walking along the lakeside. Now they've found the tree. Oh, right, Henderson is wearing a climber's helmet with the torch in it. That makes it easy."

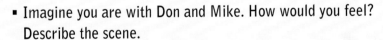

THINK

- Imagine you are with Don and Mike. How would you feel? Describe the scene.

1 make a run for it 逃逸
2 mission [ˈmɪʃən] (n.) 任務
3 accomplish [əˈkɑmplɪʃ] (v.) 完成
4 whisper [ˈhwɪspɚ] (v.) 低聲説
5 lad [læd] (n.) 男孩

6 confirm [kənˈfɝm] (v.) 確認
7 continuously [kənˈtɪnjuəslɪ] (adv.) 連續地
8 situation [ˌsɪtʃuˈeʃən] (n.) 情況；處境
9 halfway [ˈhæfˈwe] (adv.) 到一半
10 penknife [ˈpɛnˌnaɪf] (n.) 小刀

Mike handed the night sights back.

"Sergeant," he whispered. "Is everything OK?"

"Fine, lad[5], fine," he whispered. "They're just putting the boat into the water, and Roberts is getting into it."

"That's right," I confirmed[6]. "Mike, are you ready for action?"

He reached into his box and put some things into his pockets.

"Sergeant, are you ready?" I asked.

"Oh, yes, Don," he answered happily. "I'm more than ready."

I checked that I had everything I needed—torches, knife, night sights. Mike and I synchronized our watches: 10.25.

"They're both on the island now," said the policeman, who had been watching the two men continuously[7] through his night sights. "It's time to go down to the lake."

Slowly and quietly we collected what we needed and then we led Sergeant Keddle down to the water. We each held one of his arms and took one step at a time. When we were on the path, the Sergeant and I looked through our night sights to see what the situation[8] was. Henderson was already halfway[9] up the tree. He was moving quickly.

"Look," I said to Mike. "You can see where he is from the light on his safety helmet."

For a moment all three of us watched him as he climbed higher. We could see the helmet light shining on the tree.

At that moment I took out my knife and moved down to the tree which had the boat rope tied around it. I cut through the rope with my penknife[10]. Now they wouldn't be able to pull themselves back to land.

"He's reached the nest," whispered the policeman. "Oh, my goodness!"

There was a terrible noise as the female osprey flew up from the nest calling "kew-kew-kew" over and over again. We heard the male answering her from over at Marsh Pool. Then she was quiet.

I looked through my night sights again, and watched as Henderson carefully put three eggs into a box, which he then put into a bag. After that he whistled once, and started lowering the eggs down on a long rope to Roberts who was waiting below.

"Lights, boys," said Sergeant Keddle quietly and calmly.

We checked our watches—10.43. "OK—go," I said.

I counted my way to the nearest light, and got my camera ready. I looked at my watch and counted down. Then I threw[1] the switch[2] on the first lamp, and saw that Mike had done the same. I walked the next five paces and threw the switch on the next lamp. The island was blazing[3] with light.

I took a series of photographs of Roberts holding the bag with the box of eggs in it. Then I froze[4]. A loud voice was speaking clearly. It was Sergeant Keddle speaking through a police megaphone[5]. "Steven James Roberts and William Richard Henderson remain where you are. You are under arrest[6] under the Protection of Birds Act for stealing the eggs of a protected species of bird. Anything you say may be taken down[7] and used in evidence against you."

1 throw [θro] (v.) 轉動（機器開關）（動
　詞三態：throw; threw; thrown）
2 switch [swɪtʃ] (n.) 開關
3 blaze [blez] (v.) 閃耀
4 freeze [friz] (v.) 呆住（動詞三態：
　freeze; froze; frozen）
5 megaphone [ˋmɛɡəˌfon] (n.) 擴音器
6 under arrest 被捕的
7 take down 記下

THINK

- How do you think the boys felt as they waited to switch on the lights?
- Would you like to have been doing that? Why/why not?

Roberts froze for a few moments. Then he took the eggs and ran towards the boat. He got into it, and started to pull on the rope. But nothing happened because I had the cut the rope earlier.

"Roberts," it was the policeman's voice again. "Get out of the boat. Go back to the tree. Attach the eggs to the rope. Henderson. Pull the eggs back up to you and put them back into the nest."

Sergeant Keddle's voice had such authority[1] that the two men did exactly what he said. Once he had seen that the eggs had been put back in the nest, he spoke again.

"Henderson, come down from the tree. Then join Roberts at the beach end of the island. Sit down with your hands on your heads and wait."

I watched as Bill Henderson came carefully and lightly down the tree. He walked over to join Steve Roberts who was already sitting with his hands on his head. At that moment I heard the sirens of several police cars getting closer. Soon we heard talking and saw torches flashing on the pathway[2].

"This way, gentlemen," said Sergeant Keddle to his colleagues[3] through the megaphone.

The policemen pushed a boat into the water and rowed across the lake to the island. Then they handcuffed[4] Roberts and Henderson and took them away.

Sergeant Keddle turned round. "Boys," he said, shaking our hands. "Well done. A most successful adventure[5]. Now, can I offer you a lift[6] home? We can come and clear everything up in the morning."

THINK

- How does the policeman feel at the end?
- How do you think the boys feel?

---

1 authority [əˈθɔrətɪ] (n.) 威嚴；
  權威人士
2 pathway [ˈpæθˌwe] (n.) 路；小徑
3 colleague [ˈkɑlig] (n.) 同事；同僚

4 handcuff [ˈhændˌkʌf] (v.) 給戴上
  手銬
5 adventure [ədˈvɛntʃɚ] (n.) 冒險
6 lift [lɪft] (n.)（搭）便車

1⁶ Reflections

Sergeant Keddle brought us home. Our parents were surprised to see us. Sergeant Keddle told them what had happened and they seemed both proud and relieved that we were okay.

The next morning we went back out to Redman's Pools with Sergeant Keddle. Mike and I were delighted to see that the female was back on her nest as sometimes birds can abandon[1] a nest if someone tampers[2] with it.

We collected all of our belongings[3], which the Sergeant took back in his car, and then Mike and I cycled back home, talking all the way about everything that had happened.

A week later the three eggs hatched[4]. We felt proud that we had managed to save them.

Several months later, Roberts was convicted, fined and imprisoned[5]. Henderson was only fined and given a warning.

Two of the osprey chicks grew, and fledged[6], and flew—the third one didn't make it[7], as often happens. We hope to see the family again next year.

Of course, there was a lot of media[8] coverage[9] about us, Sergeant Keddle and Redman's Pools. Sergeant Keddle got commended[10]. We were praised and criticized[11] in equal amounts. Praised for protecting the birds, criticized for not telling the proper authorities about them sooner.

Redman's Pools was made into a Local Nature Reserve, and everyone hopes the ospreys will return next year. They are already building a hide[12] near the lake and turning Redman's Farm into a visitors' and nature study center.

THINK

- Do you think the boys deserved more praise or more criticism?

---

1 abandon [ə`bændən] (v.) 拋棄
2 tamper [`tæmpɚ] (v.) 損害
3 belongings [bə`lɔŋɪŋz] (n.)
　〔複〕所攜帶之物
4 hatch [hætʃ] (v.) 孵化
5 imprison [ɪm`prɪzn̩] (v.) 監禁
6 fledge [flɛdʒ] (v.) 長飛羽

7 make it 成功完成某事
8 media [`midɪə] (n.) 媒體（medium 的複數）
9 coverage [`kʌvərɪdʒ] (n.) 新聞報導
10 commend [kə`mɛnd] (v.) 表揚
11 criticize [`krɪtɪˌsaɪz] (v.) 批評
12 hide [haɪd] (n.) 觀察野獸活動的隱密場所

Ⓐ Characters

1 Make a list of all the characters who appear in the book. Say who they are. Are there any other people who are mentioned but don't actually appear and speak?

2 Who are the main characters in *Operation Osprey*?

3 What are the main characters like? Read the adjectives in the box and decide if any of them fit the main characters and their actions. Are there other words you would like to add? Complete the table.

> responsible   irresponsible   silly   impulsive
> careless   bad   good   kind   enthusiastic
> careful   concerned   dangerous   illegal

NAME	Characteristics

4 Write about how the characters interact in the story. What are their relationships? You may want to use these words:

best friend
friend
business acquaintance
professional relationship
ally enemy

For example   *Mike and Don are best friends.*

5 Listen and number the pictures.

6 Imagine you are a journalist. Invent an interview with Sergeant Keddle. Ask and answer with a partner.

❸ Plot

7 What kind of story is *Operation Osprey*? Tick below.

_____ a adventure
_____ b comedy
_____ c ghost story
_____ d horror
_____ e murder mystery
_____ f romance
_____ g spy story
_____ h thriller

8 The person who tells the story is called the narrator. Who is the narrator in this story? Give some examples from the text to illustrate your answer.

9 The sentences below summarize the story. Put them in the correct order.

_____ a Don and Mike realize that Mr Roberts wants to steal the eggs.

_____ b Sergeant Keddle and the boys catch Roberts and Henderson.

_____ c The boys meet a business acquaintance of Don's father's unexpectedly at the pools.

_____ d The boys ask the village policeman to help them.

_____ e Mr Roberts brings Henderson to the pools.

_____ f Don and Mike make a plan to trap Mr Roberts when he is stealing the eggs.

_____ g The boys find out that a pair of ospreys are nesting at the pools.

_____ h Mike tells his friend Don that he thinks he has spotted an osprey at some nearby pools.

10 Where would you include the other parts of the story below? Why are they important to the plot?

- a) The boys watch and record Mr Roberts' preparations.
- b) The boys tell Don's father about the ospreys.
- c) Roberts and Henderson are sent to court and punished.
- d) The boys decide to keep the ospreys a secret.
- e) The boys meet Mr Roberts unexpectedly when they're setting up the lights.

11 Complete this timeline from the start of the story to the end, indicating the timing of the main events.

Redman's Pool becomes a Nature Reserve

Mike sees the osprey for the first time

12 Make a list of all the places that are mentioned in the story, and decide which are the most important ones to the action of the story, and explain why.

13 Write a full summary of the story. Make sure you use linking words like the ones in the box to connect your text.

> first   then   after that
> finally   sometime later   despite
> as soon as   next   soon   although
> the following (day/week)

ⓒ Language

14 Don and Mike text each other on their mobile phones throughout the story. Translate their messages into normal English. Use the context to help you.

Mkt 7. UGNT.

Meet at RP 5. V UGNT.

....

Think R at RP 2moro. Me 2.

....

CU

....

RU at RP?

....

....

15 Listen to these extracts and say what atmosphere the author is creating and how he does it. Take notes. For example, is it exciting, frightening, or angry? What do the people say to show how they feel?

Extract 1

....

Extract 2

....

Extract 3

....

Extract 4

....

16 Discuss the extracts with a partner.

17 Look at these lexical sets and decide why the words go together.

- a binoculars / scanned / species / list / notebook / watching

- b osprey / circled / settled / calling / took off / sitting / build a nest

- c long rope / coil / hanging / tied / undid / letting out / pulling

- d boat / plastic / inflatable / foot pump / inflate / a paddle / row / maneuvered / get out / paddled

- e Johnson Electricals / company / do business with / deal / buy / components / Sales Manager / contract / sign / meeting

- f climb / climber / safety helmet / belt / attached / climbing spikes

- g law / criminal / put in prison / fined / police

18 Without looking back at the story, write a description of either an osprey or Redman's Pools.

....

....

....

....

....

....

1 Fill in the fact file with information from the story and introduction.

OSPREY FACT FILE

Latin name

Body length

Wingspan

Color: head

Color: upper wings

Color: under wings

Food

Hunting method

Nest

Summer (countries)

Winter (countries)

Eggs

2 Choose one of the protected species below. Use the Internet to find out more about them. Write a description, and use photographs or drawings to illustrate it.

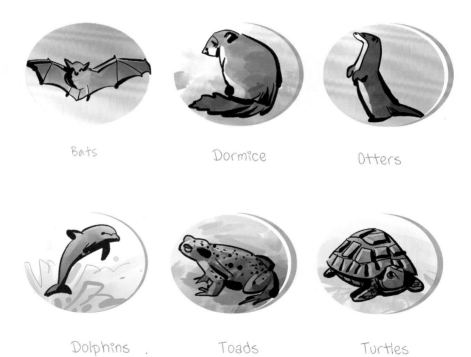

Bats

Dormice

Otters

Dolphins

Toads

Turtles

3 The RSPB has a series of webcams where you can practice your birdwatching: http://www.rspb.org.uk/webcams/ Choose one of the locations and write a report. Describe the area and what you see.

4 Read the following news report about ospreys and choose the correct word for each space.

OSPREY!
A new project for the birds

The first osprey to (a) _____ in England in more than 150 years (b) _____ its public debit in Rutland. The osprey (c) _____ was born last month and is the first success of a six-year breeding project at Rutland Water. The birds of prey almost became (d) _____  in England in the 19th century but they did survive in Scotland. And since 1997 a dozen six-week-old ospreys have been relocated every year from Scotland to Rutland Water. Experts are carefully monitoring the bird. They (e) _____ it to take its first flight in the next few weeks.

a ① born   ② live   ③ hatch

b ① has done   ② has made   ③ is making

c ① chick   ② check   ③ chuck

d ① extinguished ② extent   ③ extinct

e ① expect   ② suspect   ③ respect

作者簡介　我出生在英格蘭密德蘭區一個叫做瓦沙爾的小鎮，密德蘭區素有「黑鄉」之稱（譯註：該區為英格蘭的工業重鎮，工業污染嚴重）。我家就位於小鎮的邊緣，所以只要跨過馬路，便可以來到一處很大的公園，再走過去就是開闊的鄉間了。

我沒事時大都會去公園和鄉間玩，因而開啟了我對大自然的熱愛。十五歲時，爸媽有一次帶我去蘇格蘭露營度假，我在著名的「哥騰湖魚鷹護育中心」裡，第一次看到了和這篇故事有關的魚鷹。一年後，我加入了「皇家鳥類保護協會」，這篇故事裡的兩個男孩，也都是協會的成員。

十八歲上大學時，我認識了一位好友，他後來成為了職業賞鳥人。我們花很多時間一起賞鳥，他還教我如何把鳥從鳥巢裡安全地抓起來，以及如何把套環繫在鳥的腳上，以追蹤遷徙情況。

大學畢業後，我擔任教職，也開始拿起筆來寫詩和短篇故事。我住過義大利、科索渥、塞爾維亞，目前客居匈牙利。我是一位自由作家、教師和師資訓練員，因為工作的需要，經常到世界各地旅遊。當然，不管到哪裡，我都會遇到有趣的人事物，帶給我寫作的靈感，豐富角色和劇情的轉折。

希望這個故事能帶給各位讀者樂趣，一如我當初在寫作時那樣愉快。希望這個故事也能讓你想踏出戶外，去拜訪附近的鄉間，看看身旁發生的事物。

本書簡介　這篇講述魚鷹回到英國築巢的故事，讓人驚異。 1910 年之後，魚鷹由於遭到濫捕而絕跡，從此之後，就只有在北歐和俄羅斯的移棲地和築巢地才可以看到。到了 1945 年，終於有一對魚鷹返回蘇格蘭的哥騰湖。

皇家鳥類保護協會在小島上成立了防護所，讓這一對魚鷹可以在樹林裡築巢。在接下來的幾年，小魚鷹生了出來，可是有些蛋卻被竊。最後，哥騰湖成為鳥類保護區，人們可以在那裡觀賞到魚鷹和魚鷹的雛鳥。漸漸地，年輕的魚鷹也來到哥騰湖和蘇格蘭的其他湖泊落腳築巢。現在，每一年都有一百多對的魚鷹飛來築巢。

賞鳥人士一直在等待著第一對魚鷹能夠在英國的更南部產卵，近幾年才終於在威爾斯和蘇格蘭地區成功繁殖。

魚鷹這種鳥看上去很「壯觀」，牠們身長 50-60 公分，翅膀伸展開來可寬達 150-170 公分。讓賞鳥人士覺得有趣的是，魚鷹是吃魚的，這和其他大多數的猛禽不同。在捕食魚類時，牠們會先在湖面上的高空飛翔，然後俯衝潛入水中，在魚躍出水面之前，就用鳥爪緊緊抓住魚，然後飛離水面，回到樹枝上或鳥巢裡享用大餐。

牠們會在樹頂上用很多小枯枝來築巢，巢的寬度可達 1.5 公尺，而且每年都會返回同一個鳥巢裡。魚鷹每年都會從歐洲遷徙至撒哈拉沙漠以南的非洲地區過冬，並且在來年的四月返回築巢。

1. 相約見面

P.11

　　星期二放學後，就在我下公車要走回家時，我收到麥克傳來的簡訊。簡訊的內容很短，只有「Mkt X 7. UGNT」幾個字。我知道他的意思是要我今天晚上七點，和他在「十字架市場」碰面，他有緊急的事要跟我說。

　　這有點不尋常，因為我們平時都是在星期五放學後才碰面，然後一起計畫週末假期的賞鳥行程。所以現在一定是有什麼特別的事，一想到這裡，我就感到興奮。

　　我先介紹一下自己，我叫唐·鮑爾，今年十五歲，就讀於布魯威綜合中學。麥克（全名為麥克·彼得斯）和我同年，就讀於當地的普通中學。我們都住在密德蘭區的索雷村，從小學開始就是死黨。

　　我們從十一歲起就一起賞鳥，我想我們現在堪稱賞鳥行家，因為我們常常去賞鳥，也會閱讀賞鳥的書籍，上網研究鳥類，而且我們還是賞鳥俱樂部的會員。

P.12

想想看

•你覺得麥克在和唐碰面時，會告訴他什麼？

　　為了晚上可以出去和麥克碰面，我回到家後，便拿了餅乾和橘子汁，立刻鑽進書房寫功課。我這次寫功課比平常多花了一點時間，因為我的心老想著麥克到底會跟我說什麼，我想他一定是看到了稀有鳥類。（當然，我想簡訊一定是和鳥有關！）

　　現在是四月初，飛去南方溫暖國家過冬的鳥，現在正飛返英國避暑。在這種時刻，我們期盼著能「看見那些老朋友」，也希望能遇見稀有的訪客。

2. 得知消息

P.13

　　晚上六點四十五分，我走出家門，一路來到村子的中心地帶。索雷村是個小地方，只有一座古老的教堂、兩家酒館、一間郵局、一家食品雜貨店和幾家日常用品店。

　　這裡是上千位村民左右的家園，有一半的村民在附近的農場工作，另外一半的村民每天通勤到最近的一個大城市上班。十字架市場就位在索雷村中央的小廣場地點。

我沿路走著，向幾個熟識的人打招呼，然後坐在十字架的石製底座的階梯上。

沒多久，我就聽到熟悉的麥克的口哨聲，他模仿著田鳧的叫聲。我看到他站在對面的馬路上，於是起身向他走去。

「嗨，麥克，什麼事？」我劈頭就問。

「稍安勿躁，我們先離開人群，我再告訴你。」他神祕兮兮地回答。

我們穿過教堂的庭院，然後在一張椅子上坐下來。

「到底是什麼事？」我又問道。

「噢，你真沉不住氣。」他開著玩笑說道，但我看得出來，他自己也是興奮莫名的樣子。

P.14

我耐著性子，他終於開腔。

「我今天向學校請了一天的假。」他說：「這個星期的天氣都很好，昨天晚上刮了暴風雨，我想會有一些特別的鳥飛來附近。」

「結果有看到什麼嗎？」我問。

「我看到了一些特別的新訪客，有幾隻燕子，我還聽到了柳鶯的叫聲。後來，我又到了紅人潭。」他答道。

「紅人潭」是我們取的一處地名，那裡有三個小湖泊，湖泊四周被樹林所環繞。在一些大比例尺的地圖上，也稱呼這地方為「紅人潭」，但因為這三個小湖泊隱身在樹叢裡，所以很多人都不知道有這個地方。

我又靜靜等著他說，這時，麥克的臉浮現出一抹微笑。

「我發現了魚鷹。」他用很沉穩的口氣說道。

「什麼？」我喊道。

「魚鷹。」他簡單地再次說道。

我坐在那裡，目瞪口呆地望著他。

容我解釋一下，魚鷹是一種大型的獵鳥，以獵魚為主。當牠雙腳潛入水中，抓起一隻大魚，然後騰空躍出水面時，那幅畫面真是蔚為奇觀。

P.15

但由於魚鷹遭到濫捕，在英國一度絕跡。後來到了一九五四年，終於有一對魚鷹來到蘇格蘭的「哥騰湖魚鷹護育中心」築巢。魚鷹受到「皇家鳥類保護協會」的保護，因為有很多人想收藏牠們的蛋。如今，魚鷹遍布蘇格蘭，很多湖邊都可以看到牠們的巢。當然，人們希望不久以後在英國各地都可以看到魚鷹在築巢。

我們以前還沒有在紅人潭看到過魚鷹，我也沒親眼見過魚鷹。去年夏天，麥克專程去蘇格蘭賞鳥時就見過魚鷹了，讓我很眼紅。

「我前後觀察了一個多小時，牠從大堡嶺那邊的樹林裡飛來。當時附近野雁走得一隻不剩，我就知道這次飛來的東西一定來頭不小。牠繞著大塘飛了兩圈，停在中間那座小島的一棵松樹上，然後再朝西方飛走。」麥克說道。

接著我們一片默然——他回憶著下午所看到的畫面，而我則想著當時我正坐在教室裡上數學課，錯失了那些精彩的畫面。

過了一會兒，麥克說道：「我們明天上午要不要去紅人潭？」

「我有課啊。」我說。

「我也有課啊，跟今天一樣。」他說。

「你想魚鷹還在那裡嗎？」我問。

P.16

「你這位賞鳥人！」他說。他言下之意是說，身為一個賞鳥人，應該知道鳥類是來無影、去無蹤的，尤其是在遷徙時期。

「你到底來不來？」

「噢，噢，好吧。」我答道。我知道要是被爸媽抓到的話，他們一定會大發雷霆的。他們知道我花很多的時間在賞鳥上，沒有用足夠的時間來讀書。

3. 蹺課

P.17

我不敢蹺一整天的課，所以上午還是到了學校。我一進到學校，就假裝生病，老師只好讓我回家。

我搭公車坐回村子，感到又興奮又緊張。我在一個站牌下車，站牌旁邊就是一條小徑的入口，沿著這條隱密的小徑走下去，便可以來到那幾座小湖。我從書包裡拿出雙眼望眼鏡，把它掛在脖子上，準備隨時使用。

一如所計畫的那樣，我在紅人農場那幾棟廢棄的建築物旁和麥克碰面。我們在一扇大門前坐下，從那裡可以看到整座大塘。

「你有看到什麼嗎？」我問道。於是他就把他筆記本裡所列的那串名單唸給我聽，裡面夾雜了幾種水鳥和一些小型鳥類，而魚鷹並未列在其中。我們向大塘掃視，將眼前所見的野雁和其他各種鳥類，一一叫出種類名稱。

「我們現在繞到另外兩座湖那邊去看看。」我建議道。

我把沉重的書包藏在一個大石頭後

面，然後從大塘的北邊出發，穿過樹林，來到較小的沼澤塘。在那裡，我們又把看到的不同鳥類寫進名單上，包括灰蒼鷺。

P.18

我們在沼澤塘觀察了半個小時左右，然後在往回走的途中經過了第三座湖——木塘。當我正準備喊說魚鷹一定是離開了時，我聽到了麥克的一陣口哨聲。

「你快看！大塘的那座小島，就在左邊的那棵樹上。」他壓低嗓門喊道。

我連忙望過去，牠就在那裡——我生平所看到的第一隻魚鷹。

「哇！」我一邊喊道，一邊仔細地盯著。牠的胸口是白色的，背部是深棕色，白色頭上、一雙黃色眼睛的旁邊長有棕色斑紋。

「安靜點，笨蛋，你會把牠嚇跑的。」麥克生氣地小聲說道。

就在這時，魚鷹飛離棲息的枝頭，繞湖飛翔，發出大聲的叫聲。我們靜觀著，令我們驚訝的是，這時又飛來了另外一隻魚鷹，牠剛剛一定是棲息在另一處。

P.19

「有兩隻魚鷹。」麥克喊了起來。

這兩隻魚鷹在小湖上盤旋，不斷發出叫聲，好一會兒後才又棲落在小島的松樹上。

「太神奇了，牠們應該是在找地方築巢。」我說。

我們知道這種期待是一種奢望，所以便沒再說什麼。

我們離開這兩隻魚鷹，然後搭公車回家，一路上期盼著我們蹺課的事不會被爸媽發現。

想想看

- 唐看到魚鷹時，為什麼會那麼興奮？
- 你有過因為某件事而特別興奮的經驗嗎？那是什麼事情？
- 為什麼男孩們心裡明白，魚鷹在紅人潭築巢是個「奢望」？

4. 假期

P.20

在接下來的這個週末，想當然耳我們把所有的時間都用來賞鳥，看著魚鷹優雅的飛姿，在湖泊上演出抓魚的驚人絕技。我們的快樂全寫在臉上，因為再過一個星期，復活節的假期就要開始了。

在假期裡的每一天，我們都流連在湖邊。天未亮時，我們就迫不及待騎著腳踏車奔到湖邊。我們做筆記、繪圖、拍照，記錄魚鷹的活動情況。沒過多久我們發現到，牠們真的要開始築巢了。

我們決定不要把這件事情透露出去，因為我們知道收藏鳥蛋的人渴望把魚鷹的蛋列入收藏，即使這是違法的事。我們偶而會在紅人潭遇到釣客或遊客，但我們守口如瓶。人們也沒有注意到魚鷹，他們大概是認不出這種鳥類吧。

但最後，我們跟我爸媽說了這件事。那天晚上，我和麥克在整天觀察魚鷹之後，和我爸媽一起吃晚餐。爸媽問了很多事，想知道我們最近到底在忙什麼。

給我爸媽看。爸媽看了很感動，很讚賞我們的認真與投入。

想想看

- 兩位男孩決定把魚鷹的事當作祕密，你覺得這是個好主意嗎？
- 他們為什麼又要告訴唐的父母？這個主意好嗎？
- 如果換作是你，你會保守祕密，還是會告訴別人？

P.22

「麥克，我們要說嗎？」我一邊問，一邊將目光從麥克身上移向媽媽、爸爸。

「我們要他們先保證，一定不會把這件事情說出去。」他半開玩笑地回答。

於是我們就把整件事情說了出來，還拿出我們的筆記、圖畫、地圖和照片

5. 羅伯茲先生

P.23

假期結束後，我們回到學校上課。此時，那兩隻魚鷹的巢已經築好，就築在大塘中間那座小島的一棵松樹樹頂上。當然，我們仍會趁著每個週末和幾個放學後的晚上，跑去觀察牠們。現在，白晝愈來愈長了。

一個星期六，我們在小徑附近的馬路旁，意外發現那裡停了一輛白色的廂型車。當我們騎著腳踏車沿著小徑來到紅人農場時，看到了一位中年男子站在那裡打量著我們。當我們騎到他旁邊時，他開腔道：「哈，原來是兩位鳥類專家來啦。」

麥克和我互看了一眼，有一種疑惑不安的感覺。當我們用鎖鏈把腳踏車綁在柵欄上時，那個人又說道：「我想是唐和麥克吧，不知哪位是唐，哪位是麥克。」他說完後便笑了起來。

他的目光在我們兩個人的身上移來移去，等著我們開口說話，但我和麥克站在那裡不發一語。

「你們之中……誰是唐？」我站在原地點了點頭。「我要感謝你爸爸，把你們那個神奇的發現告訴了我。」

我的臉立刻漲得通紅，心情為之一沉，麥克則生氣地瞪著我。我那個老爸怎麼這麼笨，竟然把這件事情洩露出去。那個男人緊盯著我們，好像很關心我們會對他有什麼樣的反應。

P.24

「我想你們一定忙著做研究，所以請不要擔心我，我只是四處逛逛，看看可以瞧到些什麼。對了，我是羅伯茲先生，很高興遇到你們。」他說完便轉過身去，開始走向湖泊。

他走開約莫一百公尺遠後，麥克轉向我，說道：「你知不知道這是怎麼一回事？你爸為什麼要告訴他？他是誰？想要做什麼嗎？」

「麥克，我哪裡曉得。」我也有些火了，「我知道的又沒有你多。」

那一天接下來都顯得很緊張，湖泊的各個地方時而都可以看到羅伯茲先生的身影，他帶著雙眼望鏡和照相機，對著魚鷹一邊觀察、一邊拍照。在正中午左右的時候，他踱到我和麥克正坐著賞鳥的地方。

「我要走了，多謝你們的幫忙。唐，代我問候一下你爸。」他說。

「什麼幫忙？」他走了之後，麥克問：「我們根本什麼忙都沒幫他。我不喜歡這個人。」

「我也不喜歡。你先不要擔心，我回家問我爸，看他到底是誰。」我回答道。

想想看
• 男孩看到羅伯茲先生時，有何感覺？
• 羅伯茲先生是誰？你想他有何企圖？

6. 老爸的解釋

P.25

那天晚上回到家後，我真是氣炸了。我覺得老爸背叛了我們，虧我們這麼信任他，他竟然把魚鷹的事告訴別人。當時他正和媽媽坐在廚房裡吃晚飯，我砰砰碰碰地闖進廚房。

「爸，你到底做了什麼好事？羅伯茲先生是誰？為什麼你要把魚鷹的事告訴他，我們不是要你別說出去的嗎？」我喊道。

爸媽露出困惑不解的表情盯著我看。我平常很少這樣氣沖沖的。

「抱歉。」我說道，並竭力讓自己平靜下來，「今天有個叫羅伯茲的男人跑到紅人潭來，說是你跟他講我們和魚鷹的事的。」

爸爸顯得有點難為情，媽媽則面帶憂慮。

P.27

「他是我在商場上的朋友，我們午餐時常會在一起閒聊。」老爸於是開始解釋起來：「那天我碰巧提到你很喜歡鳥，他說他也很喜歡賞鳥，所以我們就聊了起來。我很抱歉，我知道不應該把魚鷹的事告訴他，但因為你和麥克所做的事讓我覺得很驕傲，所以我就講過頭了。」

「可是爸，你知道這件事事關重大，是不能說出去的！」我繼續說。

「親愛的，別擔心。」媽媽說：「我相信他和你一樣，只是喜歡賞鳥罷了。」

「最好是這樣。」我生氣地說完後就走出廚房，上樓走回自己的房間。

想想看

- 你有沒有對父母發過火？那是什麼時候的事？為什麼？
- 為什麼麥克會這麼擔心羅伯茲先生知道有魚鷹的事？

7. 再次狹路相逢

P.28

第二天，也就是那個星期天，我和麥克在紅人潭待了一整天，而且從那個時候起，我們每個晚上都會去報到，但那輛白色的廂型車和羅伯茲沒有再出現過，甚至接下來的週末也都沒有看到他的蹤影。然而到了星期一，當我在上學途中搭公車經過時，卻看到了那輛廂型車就停在馬路旁邊，於是我立刻一躍而起，拉了車鈴下車。

當下我決定不走通往紅人農場的那條主要小徑，那是我們慣常走的路。我決定改走繞過大堡嶺後面那條很少人走的小路。這條小路通向大塘和沼澤塘之間的樹林，讓我有個優勢，可以藏身在地勢較高的樹林裡俯視大塘而不被發現。

我用雙眼望遠鏡環顧四周，沒有發現羅伯茲先生的蹤跡。我看到其中一隻魚鷹正棲息在巢裡，牠大概就是那隻母的，而另外一隻則停在附近的一個枝頭上吃

著獵來的魚。這時我看到一道藍色的閃光向左邊走去，發現羅伯茲先生正沿著大塘邊走著，肩上還背著一個很大的藍色塑膠袋。

他在最接近小島的岸邊停了下來，然後打開塑膠袋，開始動手幹起活來。因為被灌木叢和樹木擋著，所以我看得不是很清楚，於是我立刻靜靜地轉移陣地，找了一個視野較佳的地方。

P.29

想想看

• 你想羅伯茲先生的袋子裡帶了什麼東西？

眼前這一幕讓我嚇了一大跳，羅伯茲先生竟從藍色塑膠袋裡取出了充氣的塑膠小艇，然後用一個腳踏打氣筒充起飽氣來，準備划著氣艇到魚鷹所棲息的小島上！

他花了十分鐘左右的時間幫小艇充氣，然後把小艇放到水面上，隨後抓著塑膠袋爬進小艇裡。小艇很小，空間剛好塞滿他和塑膠袋，接著他拿出一個小小的塑膠划槳，開始划過湖面往小島前進。

公魚鷹這時發出了啾啾的刺耳警告聲，然後飛離枝頭，在附近來回打轉。母魚鷹則待在巢裡，不安地四處望著，但身體並沒有移動。公魚鷹後來飛走，棲落在湖泊另一邊的一棵樹上，當小艇逐漸挨近小島時，公魚鷹仍在那裡警戒著。

羅伯茲先生輕巧地划著小艇來到小島的東側，然後爬上一處遍佈著小碎石的岸邊。之後他把小艇拖離水面，一路往四棵大樹那裡走去。這段路不好走，因為整座小島都被濃密的灌木叢給覆蓋住，我看著他一路往幾株大樹那裡奮力邁進，邊走邊踩踏著灌木叢。

P.30

我看得很焦急，這個人到底是要做什麼？當他到達幾株大樹那裡時，便抬起頭來仰望，想弄清楚鳥巢是蓋在哪一棵樹上。接下來他賣力穿過灌木叢，轉到小島上剛好面對到我的那一側，也就是他剛剛過來的方向。

他朝著我的方向這邊看過來，我屏住呼吸，一動也不敢動，希望他看不到我。之後，他走回小艇，從藍色塑膠袋裡拿出東西，我一開始看不清楚那是什麼東西，但很快就看出來那是長繩子。難道他打算爬上那棵樹？

接著，他帶著繩子走回築有鳥巢的大

樹邊，把繩子的一端綁在樹根附近，然後連拉了幾次，檢查是否牢靠。之後，他再一次穿過灌木叢，一邊走、一邊沿路放下繩子，直到來到小島的湖畔，那裡正好向著我。他用雜草把繩子覆蓋住，從我的位置無法看到繩子，最後他把繩子的尾端懸在湖水邊。

接下來，他回到塑膠小艇那裡，把小艇拖進湖裡，然後跳進裡面，用槳划向湖邊懸盪著繩子的地方。他鬆開繩圈，然後慢慢划回位於我下方的陸地，任由繩子留在湖水裡。

P. 32

他回到小徑上之後，把小艇拖離湖面，然後把繩子的一端綁在湖邊的一棵傾斜的樹幹上。接著他分別在樹的左右兩側查看，確保繩子不會被人發現。最後，他從袋子裡拿出發光的黃色黏性膠帶，在樹幹上黏了一小塊膠帶，然後往退了幾步，欣賞著自己的傑作，我看到他的臉上露出一抹笑意。

之後，他收起小艇和藍色袋子，沿著大塘的岸邊快步走回紅人農場。我納悶他為什麼沒有把小艇的氣放掉，而只是把小艇折一折，塞回袋子裡。

走回農場後，他把小艇藏在一間農舍裡，然後關上門，再從口袋裡掏出一把小掛鎖，把門鎖上。接著，他又在門上貼上一塊黃色膠帶，然後才離開。

我待在原地想了許久，想釐清眼前所看的這一切。首先，他把繩子沉在水中，這是要做什麼用的？有可能是用來把他拉過湖面的，這會比划槳快。再者，他把小艇留在紅人農場，這可以替

他省下十分鐘左右的時間。而他在樹幹和門上都貼上黃色膠帶，應該是做記號，方便下次來找。我想的越多，事情就越明顯：他一定是要來偷魚鷹蛋的。

P. 33

一想到這裡，我就憤憤不平。他怎麼可以這樣做？我很氣自己，是我和麥克把事情告訴爸爸的，所以羅伯茲先生才會知道，這是我們的錯。既然是我們的錯，我們就要確保蛋會平安無事。

我看了一下手錶，才上午十點，但我決定不去學校了。我拿出手機，發出一封簡訊給麥克：Meet at RP 5. V UGNT（下午五點在紅人潭見，十分緊急）。

想想看

• 如果你是唐，你會怎樣做？
• 還有什麼事是唐可以做的嗎？

我往下走到小徑上，看著羅伯茲先生親手做的作品——那根繩子和黃色膠帶。我很想把膠帶撕掉，然後把繩子鬆開，但後來決定還是等麥克過來再說。接著，我又走到農場的房舍，檢查那扇門，門上掛著一付閃閃發亮的新鎖，並且貼著黃色膠帶。我想了一下，不知道羅伯茲先生為什麼會相中這個農舍，後來我看到其他兩三間房舍裡面都堆滿了垃圾，所以就猜想應該是這間農舍比較乾淨的緣故吧。

P.34

在麥克抵達之前，我還得等待六個小時，於是我坐下來記錄魚鷹的行為。我看到公魚鷹抓了一條魚，然後把魚送回給在巢中孵蛋的母魚鷹，牠們的蛋是很稀有珍貴的。當公魚鷹飛回之際，母魚鷹發出了口哨般的叫聲，然後挺起身子，伸展開一對小翅膀，不斷拍打著，然後開始進食。這時公魚鷹又飛開了，飛到下一棵大樹那裡，棲息在牠平時最喜歡逗留的那根枝頭上。

我開始陷入沉思，怎麼會有人想要來偷牠們的蛋，破壞這麼美好的一切？難道就只為了把蛋擺進玻璃箱，然後偶而拿出來看一看？我覺得這種事實在荒謬，更何況這是違法的行為。我們是不是應該報警？我得先跟麥克討論看看。

想想看

• 你認為唐和麥克應該把羅伯茲先生的事告訴警方嗎？

8. 麥克得知壞消息

P.35

下午五點一過，麥克的人就來了。我把所發生的事告訴他，他神色憂慮了起來。我們先去了農舍，接著到綁有繩子的大樹那裡，我還把繩子從水裡拉出來給他看。

「你覺得我們應該怎麼做才好？」他問道。

「我也不知道。」我回答道：「起初我是想切斷繩子，把槳扔掉，把小艇弄個大洞，但後來我想還是等你過來再說。」

「謝啦。我想最好的方式是在他下手時當場活捉，我們要拍些照片，握有證據是很重要的，然後我們再報警，交由警方處理。」麥克說。

「這個主意不錯，但我們得一直守在這裡。他之所以會趁上午來，就是因為知道我們要上學，那麼他在下午和週末時就不會過來，那是我們活動的時間。還有，他清晨一大早的時間也可能過來，那時候這裡不太會有人。」我回答。

「沒錯，你說得對。你今天早上是幾點過來的？」麥克說。

P.36

「我想想看……，我是在七點四十五分坐上從索雷鎮出發的公車，預計八點半到達學校，所以我想大概是八點左右到這裡的，對吧？」我回答道。

- 針對羅伯茲先生的所作所為，為什麼「握有證據」對兩位男孩來說很重要？

「奇怪的是，他怎麼沒想到我們可能會從公車上看到他的廂型車？看來他一定不是本地人，不然一定會知道會路過，要不然就是以為你跟我上同一間學校，所以不會走這條路。他是哪裡來的人？」麥克說道。

「我可以問我爸，他一定知道。」我回答。

「這主意不錯，看能不能找出一些蛛絲馬跡。不過不要再怪你老爸了，是我們自己要跟他講的，是我們自己的錯。」麥克說。

「這我知道啦。不要讓保羅伯茲先生得逞，就全靠我們了，這樣我們也才能將功贖罪。」我回答。

「我同意。我們現在先拍照，把繩子、黃色膠帶、農舍和掛鎖拍起來，好當作證據。我們先讓現場維持原樣，在旁監視就好。」麥克說。

P.37

「沒錯，麥克，但這表示我們白天要有人留守在這裡，他會在白天過來架設裝備。還有，顯然他需要可以爬上鳥巢的工具，那可有的他爬了——要爬十二公尺耶。」我說。

「沒錯。明天我會來，之後我們輪流蹺課。白天時我們就用簡訊保持聯絡，放學後五點在這裡碰面。」麥克說。

「好。我們現在就來拍些照片。」我附和地說道。

想想看

- 你覺得這兩位男孩所做的事是正確的嗎？

9. 羅伯茲先生的底細

P.39

那天晚上，我在和爸爸一起看電視時，趁機問了他羅伯茲先生的事。

「唐，我跟他也不是很熟啦。他在強生電子公司工作，和我的公司有生意上的往來。他是業務經理，我和他談過生意，想跟他們買我們公司需要的電子零件。」爸爸說。

「他是哪裡人？」我問。

「他的公司在萊斯特，但我不知道他是不是萊斯特人。」爸爸說。

「你就知道這麼多嗎？」我失望地問道。

「我再想想看……，我們一起吃飯時談到了……除了鳥之外，我們還談到了……足球、一點點政治、還有我們這一行的事……，就飯局上一些很平常的閒聊。」他說。

「你有沒有辦法知道他住在哪裡？」我問。

「這應該是沒辦法。這種事怎麼問呢，對不對？我的意思是，總不能打個電話給一個在商場上認識的人，然後問他說你住在哪裡吧！你怎麼突然對羅伯茲先生這麼有興趣？」爸爸說。

P.40

「也沒什麼事啦，」我不想透露那天上午所看到的事，「只是想說你有沒有辦法去問出來。」

我離開房間，留下滿臉狐疑的父親一個人看電視。回到臥室後，我傳了一封簡訊給麥克：「no info re R.」（沒有羅伯茲先生的任何資料）。

想想看

• 你想，唐為什麼不想把羅伯茲先生所做的事告訴爸爸？

P.41

接下來的兩天由麥克打頭陣，再換我接手。但紅人潭那裡沒有動靜，羅伯茲先生始終都沒有現身，所以我和麥克只會在放學後碰頭，觀察那兩隻魚鷹，做些記錄，然後搭公車回家。

第二天晚上，爸爸下班回家後帶回了一些消息。

「唐，我今天和你的那位朋友羅伯茲先生有講到話。」晚餐時，他笑著說道。

「講什麼？」我問道。

「他打電話給我，要談合約的事，我問他明天可不可以過來談定細節簽約，他說沒問題，因為他就住在雷汀頓，那裡就位在萊斯特和我們這裡的中間。」爸爸繼續說地。

「太好了，老爸，感激不盡。對啦……還有一件事，你知道他叫什麼名字嗎？」我說。

「知道啊，史帝夫。我不知道你為什麼想要……」爸爸說。

不等爸說完，我已經奔出房間，抓起客廳大桌子上的電話簿，衝回臥室。

幾分鐘之後，我找到了我要的東西：

史帝夫·羅伯茲
雷汀頓鎮戈登巷 24 號
43879122

P.42

我立刻抄在便條紙上，然後傳簡訊給麥克：「R lives Rittington」（羅伯茲住在雷汀頓）。

麥克很快回傳簡訊給我：「GR8」（太棒啦）。

接著我又想到爸爸剛才所說的話，於是又衝下樓去。

「爸，你剛剛是說，你明天要和羅伯茲先生碰面？」我說。

「是啊，怎麼啦？」他回答。

「你們什麼時候碰面？」我問。

「下午吧。他說早上在這一帶的別的地方有事要忙。」他說。

「謝啦，爸。」我一說完便準備離開。

「唐，你怎麼突然對史帝夫·羅伯茲這麼有興趣？」爸爸說。

「噢，沒什麼。不過不管怎麼樣，你都不要再提魚鷹、麥克和我的事，也不要說我在打聽他，拜託拜託。」我說。

「別擔心，上次是我大嘴巴，我現在什麼都不會說了。」他笑著說。

我回到房間後，傳了一封簡訊給麥克：「Think R at RP 2moro」（我想羅伯茲明天會去紅人潭，我也會去）。

雖然明天輪到麥克看守，但我也會到，麥克可能會需要人手，而且不管怎樣，我想看看接下來會發生什麼事。

麥克回傳的簡訊寫道：「CU」（到時候見）。

10. 紅人潭

P.43

星期四一大早我就從家裡溜出來，搭上早班公車，到了六點半左右，便在最接近紅人潭的站牌下車，然後往小徑走去。就在這時，那輛白色廂型車也緩緩駛至，在老地方停了下來。我躲在樹木的後面，看著羅伯茲先生走出車外，從後車門取出藍色袋子，鎖好車子，然後踏上小徑，往紅人農場出發。

我傳簡訊給麥克：「RU at RP?」（你到紅人潭了嗎？），然後把廂型車的車牌號碼和廠牌寫在筆記本上。

這時，我的手機震動了：「我在大堡嶺收到你的簡訊」。

我回傳說：「R here 2. CU 5 mins」（羅伯茲也到了，五分鐘後見）。接著我便趕往平常和麥克碰面的地方。

「嗨，你有看到他嗎？」我一坐下來便忙不迭地問道。

「嗨，唐，我看到了，他在紅人農場。」麥克回答。

麥克正透過雙眼望遠鏡盯著羅伯茲先生的一舉一動。我掏出我自己的望遠鏡，開始尋找那兩隻魚鷹。公魚鷹正停在湖泊另外一側的大樹上，母魚鷹待在巢裡。

「他在把船拖出來。」麥克說。

P. 44

我立刻把望遠鏡轉向史帝夫・羅伯茲,看到他把小艇靠在牆上立起來,然後鎖上門。接著,他看了看手錶,然後走回通往馬路的小徑上,不久便從視線中消失,只留下小艇,以及小艇旁邊的那個藍色袋子。

想想看

• 羅伯茲先生去哪裡了?

「奇怪。」我說道。

「他是不是把什麼東西忘在廂型車裡了。」麥克猜道。

不久,答案揭曉了:羅伯茲再度現身,旁邊還多了一個年輕男子。

「那是誰啊?」我開腔道。

「顯然是個共犯。」麥克回答。

我們靜靜地盯著那兩個傢伙走到農場。羅伯茲先生拿起小艇,年輕男子則拎起藍色袋子,接著便朝我們的方向走上小徑。

羅伯茲先生指出魚鷹和鳥巢給年輕男子看。他們走到貼有黃色膠帶的大樹旁,停下腳步。只見羅伯茲打開藍色袋子,拿出一根新的繩子,把它綁在小艇前方的一個鐵環上,然後把另一端綁在樹上。在做完這些動作後,他們兩個人開始交談起來,看得出來羅伯茲先生是在說明接下來要怎麼做。

P. 45

「他們在做什麼?」我向麥克耳語道。

「羅伯茲在向他說明要如何登上小島。這有好戲可看了,因為小艇塞不下兩個人。」他說。

沒多久,只見羅伯茲先生爬上小艇,從年輕男子手中接過藍色袋子,然後坐下來,撈起那條沉在水面下的繩子,又快又輕鬆地把自己拉到小島上。

「這比用槳划快多了。」我驚呼。

羅伯茲站上小島後,給了年輕男子一個姆指朝上的手勢,男子於是抓起那根綁在船前鐵環上的新繩子,把小艇拉回來。接著他也坐上小艇,鬆開綁在大樹上的新繩子,把自己拉到小島上,和羅伯茲先生會合。他跨出小艇後,兩人便合力把小艇拉上陸地。

「真聰明。」麥克說道。

「又聰明又快的方法。他們一定是想事成後立刻閃人。」我回答。

接下來他們走向魚鷹築巢的那棵大樹,他們站在樹下,邊說話邊抬頭仰望。年輕男子這時往地上一坐,便動手幹起活來。我們看不到他在做什麼,因為被灌木叢擋住了。

P. 46

後來當他站起來時,我們看到他頭上戴著黃色的安全頭盔,頭盔前方還有一盞小燈,就像礦工或洞穴探險者戴的那樣。他用手握住那條繫在身上的特殊皮帶,皮帶的另一端套在旁邊的樹幹上,但那並不是魚鷹的那棵樹。看來接下去他會舉出雙臂,把身子往後仰,用雙腳攀在樹幹的兩側,跳到樹上……不過我們很意外,因為他一直待在那裡沒有動靜。

過了一會兒，他才開始爬到離地約兩公尺的高度。他將皮帶往上移動，再用腳往上爬。

「嘿，他的鞋底一定裝有爬山專用的鞋釘，所以才鉤得住。」麥克說。

「沒錯，我敢打賭，他一定是職業的攀爬高手。羅伯茲知道自己爬不上去，所以找來了專家。」我回答。

P. 47

這時年輕的攀爬手從樹幹滑下，兩人說了不少話。之後，年輕男子從我們的視線裡消失，卸下他的裝備，然後兩人走回小艇那裡。羅伯茲先生把小艇的繩子綁到湖邊的一棵小樹上，攀爬手則坐上小艇，把自己拉回陸地。

「快！快拍些照片！」麥克說。

我們一直出神地看著兩個傢伙，結果忘了拍照片來當作證據。我們這時趕緊拿出相機，趁他們兩人把自己拉回岸上之際，拍了幾張相片。

當那兩個傢伙開始走回農場時，麥克說道：「你留在這裡。」然後一溜煙地跑掉，我還來不及問他要做什麼。

P. 48

我趁著留在原地的空檔，又用變焦鏡頭拍了一些相片。當此之際，那兩個人把裝備放回農舍，羅伯茲先生鎖上門，然後兩人便離開，一路上一直在交談著。

約十五分鐘後，我聽到麥克穿過樹林跑回來的聲音。

「你在做什麼呀？」他才上氣不接下氣地坐下，我便問道。

「我想跟過去看能不能打探到更多的消息。」他說道。

「結果呢？」我問。

「我躲在汽車附近的一棵大樹後面，偷聽他們的談話。他們明天晚上十點碰面。」他回答。

「明天晚上？」我重覆道：「要在天黑之後？」

「沒錯。白天太顯眼了，不是嗎？我是說白天可能會有人過來，會看到他們，而我們也可能會在這裡出沒，但天黑之後，他們想這裡就不會有人了。對啦，那位攀爬手的車牌號碼和車子的型號我也拿到了。」麥克說。

「幹得好，福爾摩斯！」我開玩笑地

説。我這位朋友的反應真是快，令人印象深刻。

「這沒什麼，基本常識而已，親愛的華生。」他也以玩笑回敬了我一句。

想想看

• 福爾摩斯和華生是誰？為什麼這兩名男孩提到他們？

11. 明天晚上的計畫

P.49

「我們要怎麼做？」那天下午向晚時分，麥克和我一起坐在我的臥室裡，麥克開口問道。

「我的第一個想法是，在他們下手之前就加以制止。我的意思是，我們可以把小艇弄壞，把繩子割斷。」我說。

「對，起初我也是這麼想。」麥克說。

「不過，後來我又從比較長遠的角度來看。」我說。

「什麼意思？」麥克問道。

「你想想看，」我問口道：「我敢說這一定不是史帝夫・羅伯茲這輩子第一次偷蛋，也不會是最後一次偷蛋。麥克，他是個罪犯。他可能只收藏一顆，然後把剩下的蛋以高價賣給別的蒐藏者。我們不只要制止他這一次，而且要永遠制止他。如果我們把他的工具弄壞，雖然可以保住小魚鷹，但如果讓他當場人贓俱獲，那他就要吃牢飯，或是被罰錢，甚至要關也要罰錢，而且他收

藏的那些蛋而也會被沒收，送交給博物館。這樣我們就可以確定他永遠都不能再偷蛋了。」

P.50

「唐，你想得真周到。那你有想到我們要怎麼進行嗎？」麥克說。

「我想先不要讓警方來掌控這件事，他們要是開著警車、一路大搖大擺地鳴著警笛和閃著大燈，只會打草驚蛇，抓不到羅伯茲和攀爬手的。這個作法行不通。」

「我同意。只是話說回來，我們有辦法搞定嗎？我們行嗎？」麥克說。

「不行，我們沒這個能耐。我們所能做的，就是做好周詳的計畫，這樣警方趕到時，才能很快地掌握整個事件。」我說。

「唐，看得出來你是個有點頭腦的人，」麥克笑道：「我洗耳恭聽了。」

「是這樣的，你們家去年冬天辦花園派對時，你爸不是有用到探照燈和汽車電池嗎，這些東西現在還在嗎？」我說。

「還在啊，就放在車庫裡，我前幾天還有看到。我還想，我爸大概用不到這些東西了。」麥克回答。

「那好，我們把這些東西帶去紅人潭，明天上午就把它們裝起來，讓光可以照到島上魚鷹棲息的那棵樹。」我說。

「可是這些東西很重耶，是吧，我們要怎麼帶過去？」麥克說。

P.51

「用腳踏車載過去，四個車頭燈和四個電池，你載兩個，我載兩個，應該沒問題。」我回答道：「你回家後，先把

電池充電，可以嗎？把電充飽。」

「遵命，長官！」麥克説道，用阿兵哥的方式向我敬禮，我於是笑了。

「就這樣，我們第一步先把探照燈裝上，到了明天晚上，就恭候羅伯茲和他的朋友大駕光臨小島。等攀爬手爬到樹上偷蛋時，我們就打開探照燈，趕緊拍照，然後等警察來逮捕他們。」我説。

「了解，這個計畫很好，但有一個問題：我們要上哪裡去請警察來？」麥克説。

「明天我們去村裡的派出所找老警官基鐸，跟他説明所有的事情。我們可以請他在晚上九點左右去紅人潭，然後跟我們一起守株待兔，我想他一定會協助我們的。」我説。

「那如果他想接管這件事，用不一樣的方式來處理，出動大批警力，那怎麼辦？」麥克問。

P. 52

「我想應該不會，我們都知道他這個人，從小到大就很清楚他的為人，他很自負，如果我們告訴他這件事會讓他出名，甚至還可以讓他升官的話，我想他就會照我們的方法去做。我們還要準備我們自己要用的手電筒和電池，我有一個電力很強的手電筒，你也有一個不是嗎？對了，我會向我爸借紅外線夜視鏡，這樣就可以看清楚他們的動靜。」我説。

「我們還得確保一件事：萬一他們想逃跑，也跑不掉。」麥克説：「等他們出發往小島前進時，我就繞過大堡嶺的後面跑到馬路上，就像今天上午那

樣，然後戳破他們車子的輪胎，讓他們逃不掉，然後我再跑回來，這只要十分鐘的時間。」

「麥克，這個計畫很好。沒錯，這種事最好還是由你來做，因為你跑得比我快多了，你記得帶把鋭利的小刀，用來刺破輪胎的橡膠皮。」我説。

想想看

- 你覺得告訴村裡的警官是個好主意嗎？為什麼？
- 你覺得這兩位男孩的計畫如何？你認為行得通嗎？

P. 53

「我爸的工具箱裡頭有我們需要的東西，我會把它帶過來。我們現在還缺什麼東西嗎？」麥克説。

「我們還缺衣服。我們要穿上黑色的衣服，衣服上面不可以有亮亮的東西，我們可能也要把臉塗黑，這個用湖邊的泥土塗一塗就行了。你還需要戴頂帽子，把你的金髮蓋住。」我回答。

「沒錯。我有一頂冬天用的羊毛帽，是深藍色的。」麥克回答。

「我們還得想想上學的事。」我説道。

「你何不直接來我家？我爸媽比我早出門，我們家一整天都沒人。」麥克説。

「好主意。你等一下騎我的腳踏車回家，那我明天早上到你家載探照燈和電池去紅人潭時，需要用到的東西就都準備齊了。」我説。

「沒問題，如果事情都敲定了，那我現在就回家做準備。」麥克同意説。

「我剛剛還想到一件事，我們明天會

在外面待得很晚，我們要怎麼跟爸媽說？」我說。

「這簡單。你跟你爸媽說，你要在我家過夜，而我跟我爸媽說，我要去你家過夜。我們可以說，我們放學後會直接去紅人潭，因為魚鷹的蛋快要孵出來了，我們星期六一大早要再去紅人潭時也可以這麼說，他們一定會相信的。」麥克說。

P.54

「好吧，就這麼辦了，希望我爸媽不會和你爸媽在村子裡巧遇，或是互相通電話！」我說。

我們都笑了，接著麥克就離開，騎我的腳踏車回家。

我開始打點背包，準備明天晚上需要用到的東西，我還想到要塞兩個蘋果和一些巧克力在裡面。明天有一個長長的白天和夜晚要過！

12. 忙碌的一個上午

P.55

星期五早上六點，鬧鐘響起，我立刻起床開始準備。我得穿上學校的制服，爸媽才不會起疑心。今天是一個大日子，卻什麼都不能說，還要表現得很平常，這並不容易。還好爸媽每天早上起床時，總是睡眼惺忪的，不太會注意到什麼。

我要出時，盡可能用平常的口吻說：「對了，我昨天晚上忘了說，我們今天晚上會在紅人潭待得很晚，明天一大早又要回紅人潭，所以我今晚會去麥克家過夜。我們明天晚上見啦，拜拜。」我不等他們來得及問話，就溜出了家門。

我慢慢踱到村子中央，去報攤上買了一瓶礦泉水，打算帶到紅人潭去，這趟任務想必會讓人口乾舌燥。接著，我往麥克家走去。

現在才七點四十分，平常這個時間我是坐在公車上的。

P.56

快到麥克家時，我看到他爸爸的車子正駛離車庫前的車道，然後開上大馬路。

車子開過我旁邊時，我躲進一棵大樹的後面，觀察麥克的爸媽是不是都在車裡面。他們兩個人都坐在車子裡頭。

等車子一轉過街角，我立刻快步走到麥克家。我按了門鈴，麥克便讓我進門。

「今天早上還順利吧？」他問。

「很順利，我們需要的東西都在這裡了。我剛剛看到你爸媽出門，他們沒有懷疑什麼吧？」

想想看

• 唐向父母撒謊，你想他心裡是什麼的感覺？
• 你向父母撒過謊嗎？那種滋味如何？

P.57

「什麼懷疑都沒有。現在我們要先做什麼？」他說。

「我先把學校的制服換下來，我有帶衣服來換。我想把學校的書包放在你這裡，可以嗎？」我說。

「那有什麼問題。」麥克說完便領我到他的房間。

我很快換好衣服，然後把書包和制服藏在他的床下。「現在我們就把東西扛上腳踏車，出發去紅人潭。」

我們走進車庫，麥克拔掉電池上的充電器，把電池放進探照燈裡，檢查是不是會亮。在陰暗的車庫裡頭，探照燈的光很亮。

「我昨天晚上在我們腳踏車的車後座上各綁了一個很大的塑膠水果籃，這樣才好載東西。」麥克說。

我看了看他綁上的塑膠籃，說道：「這真是好主意。」

我們各在自己的塑膠籃裡放了兩個電池和探照燈，然後把腳踏車牽到車道上。麥克鎖上門，我背上背包，然後我們就出發了。

探照燈和電池都很重，所以我們騎得很辛苦。我們平常騎去那裡只需要半個小時，這次卻騎了快一個小時。騎到大堡嶺後方的小路時，我們跳下腳踏車，然後牽著腳踏車前進，找到了一個適合監看的點。

我們先卸下電池和探照燈，然後把腳踏車藏在灌木叢的後面。

之後我們放鬆了一下，對魚鷹觀察了一會兒，儘管我們一想到接下來可能發生的事，心裡就七上八下的。

P.58

想想看

• 你曾經在某事發生之前感到很緊張嗎？跟夥伴分享當時的心情。
• 你為什麼很緊張呢？

「說起來很妙，對不對？這兩隻鳥並不知道將會發生的事情，不是嗎？」我說。

我們都啞然失笑起來。

「來吧，我們開始行動吧。我建議我們先去找放探照燈的地方，找到之後再回來搬東西。」麥克說。

於是我們往湖邊走去，討論放探照燈的地方。我們找的地方要能直接照到小島，而且不能夠被羅伯茲和攀爬手發現。最後，我們沿著羅伯茲綁上繩子的大樹兩側相中了四個地方。

挑好地點之後，我們就回去先把兩個電池搬過來。第一個探照燈裝好後，便再找第二個裝探照燈的地方。而就在我們彎過一個轉角時，竟迎面碰上了羅伯茲先生！這一撞見，我們雙方都很吃驚，不過他很快變換表情，露出一個大大的微笑。

P.59

「哈囉，孩子們，真是太好啦，我們又見面了。我只是在上班的路上順便過來，看看我們那兩位有羽毛的朋友。」他說。

「羅伯茲先生，早啊。」我勉強擠出這幾個字來。

「你們星期五上午不是應該在學校裡的嗎？」他邊問邊輪流盯著我們瞧。

「這個……是……」我努力想回答。

「我們今天放假，今天學校特別放假。」麥克撒了個謊。

「原來如此。你們帶著汽車電池要做什麼？」他問。

「這個……呃……我們……打算明天錄些音，」我撒謊道，「所以趁著今天先把電池帶過來。」這個謊言慢慢圓了起來。

「你要是有興趣，明天可以過來看看。」

「這個……我明天會有點忙。謝啦，我沒辦法來。」羅伯茲先生說。

「真可惜，很好玩的。」我說。

「也是，一定很好玩。這個……你們今天會在這裡待很久嗎？」他說。

「不會。大概再待個幾小時就要走了。我們跟一位朋友借了錄音機，今天下午要去拿。」我回答。

P.60

「噢，那很好……，這個……那

好……這個我要走了，很高興又遇到你們……，祝你們錄音順利。」他說。

「謝謝你，羅伯茲先生。」當他轉進小徑時，麥克說道。

麥克和我在那裡站了好一會兒，看著他在小徑上走向大馬路。接著，我們遠遠聽到他發動車子的聲音，以及車子很快開走的聲音。

想想看

• 和羅伯茲先生不期而遇，唐和麥克會有什麼樣的心理反應？
• 你有過不期而遇的緊張經驗嗎？是什麼時候的事？你當時感覺如何？你如何應變？

「好險啊！差一點就穿幫了。」麥克說。

「是啊！想想看，如果我們是在裝探照燈時剛好被他撞見的話，那我們要怎麼解釋啊？」我說。

「不過你真厲害，撒起謊來臉不紅、氣不喘的。看你一臉不苟言笑的樣子，連我都要信以為真了。錄音，哇，虧你想得出來。」他說。

我們又笑了。

「我本來也不知道要怎麼回答，就突然想到的，好險！我們還是趕快行動吧，我們浪費了不少時間。」我說。

P.61

「沒錯，」麥克在我拿起電池時，說道：「你想他今天早上為什麼會跑來這裡？」

「可能只是來檢查一下，確保今天晚上可以順利進行。」我回答。

「我想也是。」他說。於是我們開始行動。

在接下來的一個小時裡，我們把四個電池和探照燈都裝好，並檢查它們會不會亮。探照光的亮度很強，在陽光下也看得到燈光。接著我們從小徑上做檢查，確保探照燈不會被看到。

「現在就只剩下一個問題了，」我們在完成安裝之後，麥克說道：「晚上黑漆漆，我們要怎樣看到他們兩個人？我們不能用手電筒，不然很快就會被他們發現，夜視鏡也是一樣。我們藏好身之後，就不能再使用夜視鏡了，不然他們會看到紅光。」

「你說的沒錯。」我說道，想了一會兒。「我知道了，我們可以算腳步，看從藏身地點走到探照燈需要走幾步。我

負責開右邊的兩盞探照燈，你就負責打開左邊的那兩盞。」

我們決定就這樣做，於是我們往上走回監看處，然後仔細計算走到探照燈需要走幾步。我從監看處算起，分別要走十五步和二十步，麥克則是要走十八步和二十二步。

「還有，我們必須確認會在同一時間打開探照燈。我們來對一下錶，確定時間是一樣的。今天晚上，我們再見機行事。」麥克說。

我看了看自己的手錶，「好，就這麼辦。現在是十一點，我們騎回索雷村，去找基鐸警官。」

13. 向警察細說分明

就像英國許多小村莊的派出所一樣，派出所也成了基鐸警官的家，前廳就是他的辦公室。我們按了門鈴，等著他來應門。

「哈囉，孩子們，有什麼事嗎？」老警官打開門後說道。

「基鐸警官，我們有事情想跟你說，可以嗎？」我說道。

「好啊，孩子們，請進。」他回答道，然後帶我們走進他的辦公室。

我們進去後，他坐在自己的辦公桌上，而我和麥克端坐在辦公桌前的兩張椅子上。

「有什麼問題嗎？」他問。

於是我們把事情一五一十地告訴了他，並把我們做的記錄、地圖和照片都拿給他看，最後再把我們晚上的計畫說出來。

他站起身來，在窗前來回踱了片刻，最後轉過頭來瞅著我們直瞧。

「這種作法不合標準，」他說：「要是出了任何差池，我們都會惹上麻煩，尤其是我。」

「基鐸警官，我們每一步都計畫得很完美，而且都已經準備就緒，不會有任何閃失的，而且要是抓到羅伯茲，你只會因為表現良好得到獎勵，不會有其他的事。」麥克說。

「拜託，基鐸警官，只要抓住這個人，證明他有罪，他就再也不能夠偷蛋了。」我附和道。

這回他想了更久，然後冷不防地說道：「好吧，孩子們，就這樣做吧。」

想想看

• 你曾經跟警察報過什麼重大案情嗎？那是什麼時候的事？你為什麼要報警？

• 警官一開始時覺得他們的計畫如何？

• 你想警官後來為什麼會同意他們的建議？

「基鐸警官，謝謝你。」我和麥克異口同聲地說道，感到鬆了一口氣。

「現在我們就去看看所有的安排，不過你們先給我那兩輛車的車牌號碼，我先查一下。」警官說。

P.65

他打電話給郡警總局，請他們有進一步的消息就回撥電話給他。然後就坐下來和我們討論每一個細節，包括我們要在哪裡碰面，而且我們過程中一定要保持安靜，還有時間未到時，一定不可以把燈打開等等。我們請基鐸警官開自己的私人驕車過來，不要開警車來，並告訴他車子應該停在哪裡。

在我們討論之際，那兩輛汽車的資料也傳了過來。如我們所預期的，白色廂型車的車主是史帝夫‧羅伯茲，而我們也得知了那位攀爬手的名字了，他叫比爾‧韓德森，住在萊斯特。

「太好了，我們已經確切掌握到他們的身分和住處了，這很有利。」警官說。

我們又討論了更多的內容，把每一個環節做最後的確認，然後安排在當晚九點鐘和基鐸警官碰面，最後我和麥克告辭離開。我們騎上腳踏車回麥克家，然後吃東西填飽肚子。

「他很有個樣子，對吧？」當我們大口嚼著三明治時，麥克說。

「沒錯。他查看地圖和做計畫的樣子，感覺很專業，而且會記下每一個細節。我很驚訝，沒想到他這麼有效率。」我同意地說道。

「希望他今晚也一樣罩得住。」麥克說道。

14. 重返紅人潭

P.66

下午四點，我們騎上腳踏車，來到紅人潭，我們這一天來了兩次。其實我們不需要這麼早去，但是待在索雷村裡有風險，因為爸媽都要回家了，我們怕被拆穿。一路上我們騎得很慢，也沒說上什麼話，心裡只想著晚上可能會發生的事。

當我們抵達時，通往紅人農場的小徑上還沒看到羅伯茲或韓德森的車，這讓我們很安心，少了一個要面對的難題。我們從比較少人走的小徑進入，然後把腳踏車藏在離小路遠遠的地方。

我們來到監看處，檢查所有的裝備。一切都已經就緒，我們感到很滿意，接下來我們往下走到湖邊，對魚鷹觀察了一陣子。只見公魚鷹在湖面上盤旋了幾圈，姿態很美，然後潛進湖水裡，抓起一隻大魚，帶回巢裡給母魚鷹，接著又往沼澤塘那裡飛去。我們從過去的觀察中知道，有時牠會在沼澤塘那邊的一棵枯橡樹上棲息，而母魚鷹則會站起來，抖抖身子，展開雙翅，拍打幾次，然後開始吃魚。

P.67

我們不斷練習來回走到探照燈那裡，邊走邊計算腳步。起初我們還睜開雙眼進行，但麥克後來建議我們閉起眼睛練習，揣摩一下摸黑走路的樣子。

這還真不簡單呢，我們得記住小徑的轉彎處，才不會跌進湖裡或是撞到另一側的灌木叢。

我們決定去三座小湖那裡散散步，消

115

磨一下時間，也讓自己放鬆一下。一路上我們沒有多說什麼，除了偶而指一下兩隻魚鷹的去處，說一下感想。我們兩個人都了解，這件事是我們這輩子第一次遇到的重大事情。

今天晚上氣候宜人，微風徐徐，我們觀賞著傍晚的流霞。快到八點時，我們走回監看處。

「麥克，你要吃蘋果嗎？」我問道，然後開始啃了起來。

「謝啦。」他順手接過另一顆蘋果。我們就靜靜地吃著。

「要開始準備了。我們要弄些泥巴塗在臉上，偽裝一下。」麥克說。

我們往下走到湖邊，把湖底的爛泥巴挖出來。

「你先把泥巴塗在我臉上，我再幫你塗。」我說道。

等我們都弄好了，麥克便去接基鐸警官來。

P.68

我繼續留守，獨自面對著漸自暗了的湖水景色，陷入自己的思緒裡。我又把所需要的工具再檢查一次，把白天用的雙眼望遠鏡換成爸爸的紅外線夜視鏡，然後練習使用。我看到母魚鷹正坐在松樹的樹頂上孵蛋。我不由得想，這是一個結束，也是另一個開始，過了今晚，不管是對那兩隻魚鷹，還是對麥克、對我、對羅伯茲先生、對比爾‧韓德森，或是對基鐸警官來說，事情都會變得不一樣了。

想想看

想想看

• 為什麼男孩們要把爛泥巴塗在臉上？你覺得那會是什麼樣的感覺？
• 為什麼唐會認為：對所有的人來說，事情都會變得不一樣？你認為他的意思是什麼？

15. 夜間行動

P.69

不久，我聽到身後傳來一陣微微的騷動，接著聽到麥克的耳語：「唐，是我們。」

是麥克和基鐸警官，我們互相問候了一下，之後我很快用小型手電筒照了一下四周，好讓警官知道自己的方位。接下來，我和麥克開始向警官做說明，他很快就掌握了情況。

「很好，孩子們，現在是九點三十五分，」如果他們依照原先的安排，準時在十點鐘行動，那我們現在就要開始監視那條小徑，他們會在半個小時後出現。我自己也帶了夜視裝備，那是今天下午你們離開後，我從總局那裡訂來的。我現在可以把這一帶的地形看得很清楚，這個地點很適合監視，孩子們，幹得好。」他說。

「想要來點巧克力嗎？」我問。

他們都要了一些，於是我們便吃將起來，靜靜地享受美味。

突然，一個可怕的尖叫聲劃破了漆黑的夜色。

「天哪！那是什麼叫聲？」警官說。

麥克和我竭力憋住笑聲。

P.70

「不用擔心，那是倉鴞的叫聲，牠們的巢築在紅人農場那邊。」我說。

「沒錯，不過這可能也表示，牠們被來訪的人類驚擾到了。」麥克說。

「很有道理，年輕人，你講到重點了。」警官說。

想想看

• 你有在鄉下過夜的經驗？當時有什麼樣的體驗？你有看到或聽到什麼嗎？

• 在黑暗中使用手電筒的感覺如何？能看得多清楚呢？

基鐸警官和我都把夜視鏡對向農場，起初我一無所獲，但後來我看到了手電筒開開關關的零星閃光。

「你有看到嗎，警官？」我問。

「我看到了，唐。」他回答。

「看到什麼？」麥克問，語氣中彷彿覺得自己受到了冷落。

「有人來了，我想一定是羅伯茲和韓德森，他們正在農場的房舍附近走動。」警官接口道。

「一定是他們，他們帶著塑膠小艇。麥克，現在該你上場了，快去刺破他們的輪胎。」我說。

P.72

「好。我十分鐘後就回來。」他說。

「他要去哪裡？」基鐸警官問。

「我們要讓他們就算想逃，也插翅難飛。麥克現在就是要去刺破輪胎。」我解釋道。

「考慮得很周到，硬是要得。」警官說。

不久麥克就回來了，「任務完成啦。」他悄聲說道。

我把夜視鏡交給麥克，因為我不希望他有受到冷落的感覺。他靜靜地觀察著，小聲地說明情況：「他們現在已經來到大塘，羅伯茲扛著小艇，韓德森拎著袋子，袋子裡面裝有東西。他們正沿著湖邊行走，現在他們找到那棵樹了。噢，沒錯，韓德森正在戴上攀岩用的頭盔，頭盔上面裝了燈，這樣比較好行動。」

• 想像如果你現在正和唐、麥克
在一起，你會有何感覺？描述
一下那樣的場景。

P.73

麥克這時把夜視鏡交還給我。

「警官，一切都沒問題了嗎？」他
悄聲問道。

「沒問題，孩子，都沒問題。」他
也小聲說道：「他們正在把小艇放進湖
裡，羅伯茲現在正爬上小艇。」

「沒錯。」我確認道：「麥克，你
準備好要行動了嗎？」

他把手探進工具箱裡，掏出了些東
西，然後塞進口袋裡。

「警官，你也準備好了嗎？」我問。

「噢，是的，唐。」他回答道，語
氣顯然有些興奮，「不只準備好了，我
早就躍躍欲試啦。」

我也檢查了一下自己所需要的工具，
手電筒、小刀和夜視鏡。麥克和我的手
錶顯示出同樣的時間：十點二十五分。

「他們現在都在小島上了，」一直
以夜視鏡觀察他們的警官這時說道：
「現在到了我們前往湖邊的時候啦。」

我們輕手輕腳慢慢地收好工具，然
後我和麥克便領著基鐸警官往湖邊走
去。我和麥克各挽起警官的左右臂膀，
一個腳步、一個腳步慢慢地走。當我們
來到小徑上時，警官和我又用夜視鏡望
了一下，以掌握情況。韓德森這時已經
爬到一半了，他的動作很快。

「你看，從他安全頭盔上的燈，就
可以看出他爬到哪裡了。」我對麥克
說。

一時之間，我們三個都望向韓德森，
只見他越爬越高，我們看到他的頭燈正
照在樹上。

這時，我掏出刀子，走到他們用繩子
綁住小艇的那棵樹旁邊，把繩子割斷。
現在，他們無法把自己拉回陸地上啦。

P.74

「他已經爬到鳥巢那裡了。噢，老
天。」警官悄聲說。

那隻母魚鷹從巢裡飛了出來，不斷發
出口哨般的可怕驚叫聲。我們聽到公魚鷹
從沼澤塘那邊傳來叫聲，以呼應母魚鷹，
母魚鷹隨即安靜下來。

我又拿起夜視鏡起來看，我看到韓德
森正小心翼翼地把三個蛋放到一個盒子
裡，然後再把盒子塞進一個袋子裡。之
後，他吹了一聲口哨，開始用一根長繩

子把裝有魚鷹蛋的袋子，緩緩垂降到正在下方等候的羅伯茲那裡。

「孩子們，開燈！」基鐸警官説道，語氣沉穩而鎮定。

我們查看了手錶，現在是十點四十三分。「好，展開行動。」我説。

我計算腳步，朝著最近的那盞燈出發，並帶著相機待命。我盯著手錶，開始倒數計時。接著，我把第一盞燈的開關扭開，看到麥克也在做同樣的動作。我又走了五步路，打開第二盞燈。在燈光的照射下，那座小島被照得通明。

我趁羅伯茲握住裝有蛋盒的袋子之際，連續拍了一系列的照片。這時，我突然楞住，因為傳來了又大聲又清楚的説話聲，原來是基鐸警官正透過警用擴音器説道：「史帝夫·詹姆斯·羅伯茲，和威廉·理查·韓德森，你們站在原地，不要動。你們正在偷竊保育鳥類的蛋，現在我要依鳥類保育法逮捕你們。你們所説的每一句話都會被記錄下來，當作呈堂證供。」

P.76

想想看

- 當男孩們等著要打開探照燈的那瞬間，你想他們的心情如何？
- 你是否也想這麼做？為什麼？

羅伯茲呆立了一會兒，然後拿起鳥蛋，往小艇那裡跑過去。只見他跳進小艇，開始拉繩子，但小艇動也不動，因為我已經把繩子割斷了。

「羅伯茲，」基鐸警官的聲音又再度響起，「離開小艇，回到樹的旁邊，把蛋綁回繩子上。韓德森，把蛋拉起來，放回鳥巢裡。」

基鐸警官的聲音很有威嚴，讓那兩個傢伙乖乖地照做。等到韓德森把蛋放回巢裡後，警官又開腔了。

「韓德森，現在從樹上爬下來，和羅伯茲一起待在小島的岸邊，然後雙手放在頭上，坐在那裡等候發落。」

我看著比爾·韓德森爬下樹來，他的動作很小心又輕巧，然後走到史帝夫·羅伯茲那裡，而羅伯茲已經坐在地上，雙手抱在頭上了。就在此時，我聽到一陣警笛聲，有幾輛警車正開過來。不久，我們就聽到一陣人聲，看到手電筒的燈光閃耀在小徑上。

P.77

「各位同仁，請到這邊來。」基鐸警官用擴音器指揮同仁們過來。

那批警察把小艇推進水裡，然後划過湖面來到島上，用手銬把羅伯茲和韓德森拷住，把他們押走。

基鐸警官轉過身來，一邊握住我們的手，一邊説道：「孩子們，你們做得很好，這次的出擊很成功！現在，我可以開車載你們回家嗎？上午我們可以再回來這裡，把一切清理乾淨。」

想想看

- 警官到最後的感受如何？
- 你想兩位男孩又會做何感想？

16. 思想起

P. 78

基鐸警官把我們帶回家，爸媽看了一臉愕然。基鐸警官向爸媽說明了來龍去脈後，他們看起來很驕傲，也對我們能安然無恙的回來感到鬆了一口氣。

隔天上午，我們又和基鐸警官回到紅人潭，看到母魚鷹又回到牠的巢裡，我和麥克都感到十分欣慰。鳥巢如果受到騷擾，鳥是有可能棄巢離開的。

我和麥克把我們帶來的東西全部都帶走，由警官先幫我用車子把東西載回家，我和麥克則騎腳踏車回去。一路上，我們興高采烈地聊著所發生的每一件事情。

P. 80

一個星期後，那三顆蛋都孵化了。我們好不容易終於保住了蛋，我們為此感到自豪。

幾個月之後，羅伯茲被判了罪，不但遭到罰款，也要坐牢服刑。韓德森則是被罰錢，並在訓誡後飭回。

在那三隻幼鳥中，有兩隻順利成長，牠們長毛、飛翔，可惜有一隻未能活下來，這是常見的事。我們希望明年能夠再見到這個家庭。

當然，許多媒體都爭相報導我們的事，還有基鐸警官和紅人潭的事。基鐸警官獲得表揚，我和麥克也受到了很多讚賞和批評，毀譽各半。我們被讚賞是因為我們保護了那些鳥，我們被批評是因為我們沒有盡早通知有關當局。

後來，紅人潭被列為當地的自然保護區，每個人都希望魚鷹明年能夠再回來，所以湖泊附近已經蓋了一個賞鳥用的隱蔽所，而紅人農場也被改建成觀光及自然研究中心。

ANSWER KEY

Before Reading

Page 8-9

2 (From the top in clockwise order)
pine tree, nest, lake, osprey,
fish, island

3 c, b, d, a

After Reading

Page 82

1
1. Don Ball. Schoolboy. Interested in birdwatching.
2. Mike Peters. Schoolboy. Don's best friend.
3. Mr Roberts. Business acquaintance of Don's father. He collects eggs.
4. Mr Ball. Don's father.
5. Mrs Ball. Don's mother.
6. Sergeant Keddle. The village policeman.
7. Bill Henderson. Climber. Roberts' accomplice.
8. Mike's parents are mentioned, but they don't appear.

2 The main characters are Don and Mike and, to a lesser degree, Mr Roberts.

Page 83

5
a) 3   b) 1   c) 4   d) 2

Page 84

7 a

8 Don.

9 a) 4   b) 8   c) 3   d) 7   e) 5
f) 6   g) 2   h) 1

Page 85

10
a) After a). This part is important because the boys discover more about Roberts' plans.
b) After g). It is important because Don's father tells Roberts about the osprey.
c) After b). It is important because they are punished for their crime.
d) After g). It is important because they realize that the ospreys could be in danger.
e) After f). It is important because they manage to convince Roberts that they are setting up a sound recording.

12
Redman's Pools, Saltley, Rittington, Don's house, Mike's house, and the police station.

Page 86

14
1. Market Cross at seven o'clock. Urgent.
2. Meet at Redman's Pools at five o'clock. Very urgent.
3. I think Roberts will be at Redman's Pools tomorrow. I'll be there, too.
4. See you.
5. Are you at Redman's Pools?

Page 87

17

a) They are all to do with birdwatching.

b) They describe the ospreys' behavior.

c) They describe Roberts' actions when setting up the pulley for the boat to go to the island.

d) They describe the actions in the boat.

e) They describe the contact between Don's father and Roberts.

f) They are all to do with climbing (Henderson).

g) They describe what happens when Roberts and Henderson are caught.

Project

Page 88

1

OSPREY FACT FILE

Latin name	*Pandion haliaetus*
Body length	*50-60 cm*
Wingspan	*150-170 cm*
Color: head	*White*
Color: upper wings	*Dark brown*
Color: under wings	*White*
Food	*Fish*
Hunting method	*Dives in water and catches live prey*
Nest	*Up to 1.5 meters in width*
Summer (countries)	*Europe*
Winter (countries)	*Sub-Saharan Africa*
Eggs	*Rare*

Page 91

4

a) 3   b) 2   c) 1   d) 3   e) 1

國家圖書館出版品預行編目資料

魚鷹與男孩 / David A. Hill 著;李璞良 譯. —初
版. —[臺北市]: 寂天文化, 2012.8   面; 公分.

中英對照

ISBN 978-986-318-027-2 (25K平裝附光碟片)

1.英語   2.讀本

805.18   101014418

■作者 _ David A. Hill   ■譯者 _ 李璞良   ■校對 _ 陳慧莉
■封面設計 _ 蔡怡柔   ■主編 _ 黃鈺云   ■製程管理 _ 蔡智堯
■出版者 _ 寂天文化事業股份有限公司
■電話 _ +886-2-2365-9739   ■傳真 _ +886-2-2365-9835
■網址 _ www.icosmos.com.tw   ■讀者服務 _ onlineservice@icosmos.com.tw
■出版日期 _ 2012年8月 初版一刷（250101）
■郵撥帳號 _ 1998620-0 寂天文化事業股份有限公司
■訂購金額600 （含）元以上郵資免費   ■訂購金額600元以下者，請外加郵資60元
■若有破損，請寄回更換   ■版權所有，請勿翻印